## "I ask you all to raise a glass to my fiancée. To Marisa."

But the crowd had fallen silent. Their attention had been taken by something that parted them like Moses and the Red Sea.

Marisa followed the openmouthed stares. In the newly created gangway stood a tall, solitary figure. He was looking directly at her.

Heart suddenly racing, she felt prickles run up her spine and over her skin.

Certain she was hallucinating, she blinked hard and tried to catch her breath, fought to keep her shaking legs from collapsing beneath her.

It couldn't be.

The prickles infected her brain, reduced it to fuzzy mush. The room began to spin. Something distant smashed. She had only the faintest awareness it was the glass she'd been holding before the world went black.

## Billion-Dollar Mediterranean Brides

*Reunions sealed with a diamond ring!*

Sisters Elsa and Marisa Lopez grew up loved and wanting for nothing. Until their family came under threat from dangerous criminals intent on exploiting the Lopezes' lucrative shipping company. Their lives have already changed forever, but there's one more change they had better get ready for...when they reencounter the billionaires they've never been able to forget!

Elsa finds herself under the protection of the man she was infatuated with as a teenager, self-made tycoon Santi Rodriguez, in:

*The Forbidden Innocent's Bodyguard*
Available now!

Marisa is shocked when Nikos, whom she thought was dead, storms her engagement party, intent on claiming his heir, in:

*The Secret Behind the Greek's Return*
Available now!

# Michelle Smart

---

## THE SECRET BEHIND THE GREEK'S RETURN

HARLEQUIN
PRESENTS

# HARLEQUIN®
# PRESENTS®

Recycling programs
for this product may
not exist in your area.

ISBN-13: 978-1-335-56787-1

The Secret Behind the Greek's Return

Copyright © 2021 by Michelle Smart

This edition published by arrangement with Harlequin Books S.A.

For questions and comments about the quality of this book,
please contact us at CustomerService@Harlequin.com.

Harlequin Enterprises ULC
22 Adelaide St. West, 40th Floor
Toronto, Ontario M5H 4E3, Canada
www.Harlequin.com

**Printed in U.S.A.**

**Michelle Smart**'s love affair with books started when she was a baby and would cuddle them in her cot. A voracious reader of all genres, she found her love of romance established when she stumbled across her first Harlequin book at the age of twelve. She's been reading them—and writing them—ever since. Michelle lives in Northamptonshire, England, with her husband and two young Smarties.

### Books by Michelle Smart

#### Harlequin Presents

*Her Sicilian Baby Revelation*

#### *Billion-Dollar Mediterranean Brides*
*The Forbidden Innocent's Bodyguard*

#### *Passion in Paradise*
*A Passionate Reunion in Fiji*
*His Greek Wedding Night Debt*

#### *The Delgado Inheritance*
*The Billionaire's Cinderella Contract*
*The Cost of Claiming His Heir*

#### *The Sicilian Marriage Pact*
*A Baby to Bind His Innocent*

Visit the Author Profile page
at Harlequin.com for more titles.

# CHAPTER ONE

Nikos Manolas sat in his car shaded beneath the orange trees lining the quiet Valencian suburban street, elbow resting against the window, fist tucked under his chin. On the other side of the road ran an imposingly high fence the length of the pavement and beyond. Small intermittent signs warned trespassers against breaching it.

Nikos's narrowed gaze rested on the gate ten metres away that admitted people onto the land behind the fence. He'd watched the gate for two minutes and knew he should move on before he attracted the attention of the armed guards on the other side of it.

He'd wanted one last look. He'd had it. Time to go.

He switched the engine on and put the car into gear. Before he could make his intended U-turn, the gates opened.

He put the gearstick back into neutral. A Mercedes built like a tank slowly nosed its way through the gates and pulled onto the road. He held his breath as it passed him. The tinting of the car's windows made it impossible to identify the driver.

In his rear-view mirror he watched the Mercedes shrink into the distance and take a right at the end of the street.

Nikos rubbed his chin and then, with a burst of adrenaline, put his foot on the accelerator and spun his Porsche around.

The road the Mercedes had joined was quiet this hot mid-morning, making it easy to keep tabs. When it joined the V-21, he made sure to keep three cars between them. The deeper into the city they drove, the thicker the traffic.

It had been over eighteen months since Nikos had been in the heart of Valencia. Much of the architecture was medieval, the roads and streets narrow, but modern developments had their place too, and as he drove past the majestic Palau de les Arts Reina Sofia with its sweeping roof like a feather plume, he blinked away memories of the evening he'd taken Marisa there to watch *Tristan and Isolde*. If he'd known the so-called 'Most revolutionary opera' had been, in its essence, a romance, he'd have made his excuses and begged off. Nikos liked his entertainment to be like his affairs; frenetic and forgettable.

Not that he'd enjoyed any form of entertainment in recent times. For the past year and a half he'd lived the life of a hermit in the Alaskan wilderness, residing in a log cabin accessible only by small plane.

Readjusting to society was proving harder than he'd envisaged. He'd imagined himself returning to civilisation with a bang and throwing himself back into the old party lifestyle but in the two weeks since he'd emerged from his self-imposed exile, he'd found himself reluctant to return to the spotlight. He supposed he'd become used to isolation.

When the Mercedes indicated to turn into the huge shopping complex, his chest tightened. This had been the place Marisa liked to shop. She knew its layout better than he knew the layout of his Mykonos home.

By the time the automatic sensors had read his licence plate and he'd waved his bank card in front of the scanner, he'd lost sight of her.

It was for the best, he thought, grimacing. It had been a strange burst of sentimentality that had found him outside the Lopez estate in the first place and curiosity that found him wasting precious time tailing an old lover to an underground car park. Time to follow his original plan, to drive to the airport and resume the life he'd been forced to hide from. His plane had been refuelled, his crew ready to fly him home.

As he followed the exit signs, he caught sight of the tank-like Mercedes parked ahead. It was only as he approached it that he realised it was in a row of spaces reserved for parents and children.

He slammed his foot on the brake. The car behind him sounded its horn in protest.

Why the hell would Marisa park there?

Pulse suddenly surging, he cast his gaze around for a free space and, cursing under his breath, drove straight to the closest one, which was still a good distance away.

The distance didn't matter. Out of the car, he could see clearly enough.

What he saw made his blood freeze. Marisa, curly golden-red hair bouncing in all directions, was scooping a small infant from the back of her car.

The blood in his head defrosted into a burn in an instant.

She carefully placed the child in a buggy, strapped it in, then reached back into the car and removed a large bag which she slung on the back of the buggy.

The elevators into the complex were directly opposite where Nikos had parked. In silent horror, he watched her stride towards them. He needed to hide. One slight turn of her head and she would see him.

But he couldn't move. Couldn't wrench his gaze from the lover he'd vanished from and the child—baby—he'd had no idea existed.

Marisa Lopez scrunched a face at her appearance. Should she leave her hair down or pin it up? Yes, to the former and yes to some under-eye concealer. Her light golden skin had become so pale and the rings under her eyes so dark she resembled a corpse. The black dress she'd chosen to wear only enhanced the effect, a point reinforced when her sister, Elsa, walked into her dressing room and burst into laughter. 'I suppose funeral chic beats aubergine chic.'

'Don't,' Marisa muttered. Only vanity had made her return the aubergine-coloured dress. It had clashed horribly with her red hair. This black dress, though horrendously unstylish, was marginally more flattering colour-wise.

Elsa stood behind her, wrapped her arms around Marisa's waist, groped for her hands and rested her chin on her shoulder. Their eyes met in the mirror. The contrast between them had never been so stark. Elsa shone with good health and happiness. Her eyes, though, brimmed with concern. 'Are you okay? You don't look well.'

Marisa opened her mouth to assure her sister all was well but the lie refused to form.

'I can't do this.' The words expelled in a puff.

A line cleaved Elsa's brow.

'I can't marry Raul,' Marisa whispered, and squeezed her sister's hand tightly for support as the truth of her feelings, which had swirled inside her like steadily thickening soup for so long, suddenly solidified into truth. In a stronger voice, she repeated, 'I can't marry Raul.'

There. She'd said it. Finally admitted it.

'You were right.' Her spine straightened and her lungs inflated as she spoke. 'I keep thinking about what you said the other day about not trusting him and you're right. He lied to me. Raul doesn't want to be a father to Niki. He only wants the business.'

Marisa's relationship with Raul was very much one of convenience brought about by the circumstances that had seen her world implode when a vicious cartel had targeted her family's shipping company to smuggle their drugs around the world.

Her parents' refusal to comply with their demands had resulted in her father's murder.

This had come only a few short months after Marisa's lover had drowned and she'd discovered she was pregnant.

Up against a network of brutal crooks with her father dead, the multinational family business passing into her hands, a fatherless newborn baby to love and nurture, her sister in a different country and her mother a wounded soul, Marisa's desperation for help had found her arranging a marriage with Raul Torres, a man she knew socially who ran a business of a similar kind to Lopez Shipping.

She'd been upfront about what she wanted: a father for her son and help running the badly neglected family business.

She'd chosen Raul because she'd believed he was one of the good guys. Believed they had what it took to make a good team. Believed he would make a good father to her fatherless son.

Belief had differed greatly from reality.

A month ago, the cartel had discovered the Lopezes were working with international authorities against them and hatched a plot to kidnap Elsa from her home in Austria. Santi, a man who'd been practically raised a Lopez, had taken Elsa into hiding. Marisa, her son and her mother had stayed in their heavily guarded estate, terrified for Elsa and essentially under siege. Then, two weeks ago and after fifteen months of hell, the cartel were finally defeated. It took a huge international effort to bring them down; private security forces teaming up with worldwide security organisations and culminated in a co-ordinated swoop of arrests across twelve countries.

'I keep thinking about what you said about the cartel and you were right about that too,' Marisa said. 'Raul offered us no protection at all. He abandoned the baby he swore he loved to his fate.'

And that, along with his increasingly obvious indifference to her son, was unforgiveable.

Slipping her hand from Elsa's, she rubbed her forehead. 'What am I going to do?'

'End it.'

'I know that. I mean *how* am I going to end it?' She stepped closer to the mirror and stared at her reflection, stared at the ugly dress her subconscious had chosen for her. Her gut had known before she did that she couldn't marry Raul.

'Call him. Do it now,' Elsa urged.

She found a smile. 'I can't break up with him an hour before our engagement party. That would be like poking a hornets' nest. This family doesn't need more enemies.'

Raul wouldn't tamper with the brakes of her car like the cartel had done to her father, or drown her dog, or plot to kidnap her sister, but Marisa had learned in their time together that the man she'd chosen to marry out of desperation had a strong streak of narcissism and an unlimited capacity for grudge-holding. He knew enough secrets about Lopez Shipping to ruin them.

'Well, don't wait too long,' Elsa warned.

'I won't,' she promised. Now her mind was made up, she'd do it as soon as possible. She managed another small smile. 'Although, with luck, this dress might make *him* decide to end it.'

Leaving the dressing room, Marisa walked through her bedroom then tiptoed into the dark adjoining nursery.

Her heart swelled as she peered into the cot. Her son, her heart, her life, was fast asleep, his little chest and podgy belly rising and falling. She kissed her fingers then gently placed them to his silky-soft cheek.

How could anyone look at this child and not feel the compulsion to love and protect him?

She picked up the photo on the cabinet beside the cot, the swelling of her heart sharpening as she gazed at the wry smile of her son's father. Nikos. The love of her life.

Dead.

Hot tears stung the back of her eyes and she hurriedly blinked them back before kissing Nikos's face and placing the photo back on the cabinet.

His memory lived as an ache in every beat of her heart. Only by nestling her love and grief deep inside her and holding it tight until darkness fell and she was alone to purge the anguish of his loss, had she learned to get through the days. The pain never seemed to lessen.

After taking a moment to compose herself, she left the nursery through the main door and knocked on the door opposite. Estrella, their housekeeper, opened it. Estrella had worked for the Lopezes since Marisa was eight and had happily agreed to babysit for the night.

'We're leaving now,' Marisa said, wringing her fingers together. 'Can you check the baby monitor's working for you?'

The room she'd put Estrella in was so close to the nursery she'd hear him sneeze before the monitor picked it up.

Marisa hated being parted from her son. Since his birth, she'd only left him for a handful of evenings, and a few hours here and there when it had been absolutely necessary for her to attend work in person. This would be the first time she'd left him alone with anyone but her mother and the first time she'd left him for a whole night.

'It's working fine.' Estrella held the baby monitor to her ear. 'I can hear his breathing.'

Marisa resisted the impulse to yank the monitor from her hand and listen for herself. She knew she was a paranoid first-time mother but she defied anyone to walk in her shoes and not be the same.

'You promise to call if there's any problems?'

'There won't be any problems but I promise.'

'I'll be back by ten in the morning, at the latest.'

'There's no rush, so take your time.' Estrella gave a wide, sympathetic smile. 'Enjoy having a lie-in.'

The thought alone made the nausea in her belly bubble afresh. Marisa *liked* the early-morning closeness with her baby while the rest of the household slept.

It was just for one night, she reminded herself. In the morning she'd be back home with her son and would cuddle up with him and plan how to end her engagement without provoking Raul's vengeance.

The exclusive hotel's staff had done a fabulous job of turning its function room into a glittering party pad. The two hundred guests chatting and dancing had a constant flow of champagne and canapés, the bar at the far end plentifully staffed so no one had to wait long to be served. The world-famous DJ played a medley of tunes to suit all ages and tastes and judging by the smiles, everyone seemed to be enjoying themselves. Everyone except Marisa.

Her gaze kept falling on Elsa and Santi, glued to each other's sides. They'd finally admitted their love for each other two days ago. Marisa had known for years that the two of them were meant for each other but suspecting something and seeing that love bloom before her eyes had been both heart-warming and heart-wrenching.

She had loved like that once. Loved with the whole of her heart.

Swallowing the ache, she let Raul drag her around the room to welcome their guests together and tried to curb her irritation at his annoyance every time she checked her phone for messages from Estrella.

How had she ever thought he would make a suitable husband for her and a good father for her son? She must have been mad.

No. Not mad. Frightened. Overwhelmed. Likely suffering from postnatal depression.

Once he started chatting with a group of his golfing friends, Marisa escaped his clutches and found her own friends, a bunch she'd been to school with and remained close to.

Her respite lasted only until the end of the DJ's first set.

Raul took her by the arm and steered her to the raised dais. He wanted to make a speech. Of *course* he wanted to make a speech.

Knowing she had no choice but to go along with it, she snatched another flute of champagne from the tray of a passing waiter and climbed the steps.

The music stopped. Raul took the prepared microphone and called for everyone's attention. The dance floor filled, their guests eager to hear what he had to say.

He held her hand tightly. The feel of his skin on hers made her flesh crawl.

'Thank you all for coming tonight and for your understanding at the postponement,' he said. Their party should have been held two weeks before but the takedown of the cartel and the danger it had put Marisa and her family in had forced them to postpone. 'It certainly wasn't through choice but as you know, recent events took the decision out of our hands. This has been a difficult time for me and my future wife, and your support has been appreciated.'

Marisa almost choked on her champagne. Luckily Raul was too busy basking in the applause to notice. She loved how he made it sound as if it had been a difficult time for them as a couple when the truth was the coward had hidden away until it was all over.

'I ask you all to raise a glass to my fiancée. To Marisa.'

But the crowd had fallen silent. Their attention had been taken by something that parted them like Moses and the Red Sea.

Marisa followed the open-mouthed stares. In the newly created gangway stood a tall, solitary figure. He was looking directly at her.

Heart suddenly racing, prickles ran up her spine and over her skin.

Certain she was hallucinating, she blinked hard and tried to catch her breath, fought to keep her shaking legs from collapsing beneath her.

It couldn't be.

The prickles infected her brain, reduced it to fuzzy mush. The room began to spin. Something distant smashed. She had only the faintest awareness it was the glass she'd been holding before the world went black.

Nikos cut through the stunned silence to bound up to the dais where that idiot Raul hovered over the prone Marisa, doing absolutely nothing.

The complete shock at Nikos's appearance meant no one was capable of stopping him from checking her pulse, satisfying himself that she was alive, then scooping her into his arms.

'Excuse me,' he said as he carried her through the still-frozen crowd. 'She needs air.'

Her large brown eyes opened. Fixed on him. Widened. Blinked. Blinked again. She whimpered.

A waitress opened the double doors so he could sweep a now struggling Marisa out of the room. Her hand pushed at his chest but her movements were too sluggish to be effective. The whimpering was growing. It cut through him. It was the sound a wounded puppy made.

A member of the hotel's concierge team hurried to them. 'Can I call a doctor for you, sir?'

'Not necessary. She fainted—a shock, nothing serious. Can you get the elevator for me?'

'Certainly.'

The concierge pressed the button and the elevator door opened.

'Top floor,' he commanded, stepping inside with her. Marisa had stopped struggling and gone limp. Her eyes were screwed tight like a child trying to make itself invisible to a monster.

He'd never meant to scare her and neither had he intended to make such a grand entrance.

When the birth certificate of his son had been presented to him earlier that day, Nikos had been collected and analytical in his response. The mental preparations he'd made for a positive result greatly aided this mindset. Remaining dead to Marisa was no longer an option. Allowing her engagement party to go ahead was not an option either, and he'd set off to Valencia immediately. He'd called the hotel on the drive to the airfield, certain all the rooms would be taken, and had been surprised to find the penthouse still available. Surely the happy couple would be spending the night in it?

How happy were they? How happy was *Marisa*?

He'd done his research on Marisa's fiancé during the flight back to Valencia. A few phone calls with mutual acquaintances—explaining his return from the dead had been dealt with by giving promises that he would explain in person when he next saw them—and he'd learned Raul's only attribute was that he was rich. One friend quoted him as 'an untrustworthy snake'. That had been the most positive of the opinions.

At the top floor he shifted her position to free a hand and pressed his thumb to the security box. Inside the suite he laid her loose body carefully on the sofa and took a step back to look at her properly for the first time in eighteen months.

What on earth had possessed her to wear such an unflattering dress to her own engagement party? The Marisa he'd dated had a love of fashion. This dress was something the old women of Mykonos would wear. And where was the make-up she loved to wear? Whenever he'd told her she didn't need it, she'd laugh, thank him, then trowel it on until every freckle was masked and her eyes, lips and cheeks shone with unnatural colour. Now, all her freckles, faint though they were, were on display, and his chest tightened to remember how he'd adored waking to this bare face.

She didn't move a muscle under his scrutiny. He suspected she was playing possum.

Shock at his resurrection he'd learned in recent days meant varied extreme emotions. He'd give her a minute to compose herself.

Truth was, he could do with a moment of composure too, and his suite's bar was fully stocked.

He selected an eighteen-year-old single malt, unscrewed the lid and poured a hefty measure into a crystal glass. As he took his first sip, he sensed movement behind him.

Turning, he found Marisa only a foot from him.

He took another, larger drink to burn through the lump that had formed in his throat and held her silent stare.

Her head tilted slowly from side to side as she gazed at him through wild, wide brown eyes. Her plump lips were pulled in a straight line. She was breathing heavily through her pretty nose. With her golden-red tangled mass of frizzy curls—another curious thing: the Marisa he'd dated had used every product known to humanity to prevent frizz from forming—she had the look of someone sizing him up, someone…

The word 'rabid' flashed through his mind.

Marisa stared at the ghost before her, too scared to blink for fear he'd disappear.

Since she'd woken from her faint, secure but

so *frightened* in his arms, the only thought in her pounding head was that this couldn't be real.

Nikos was dead.

*Dead.*

She'd mourned and cried herself to sleep every night for eighteen months. She'd woken every morning with a throbbing ache in her heart that time hadn't even begun to heal. She'd carried his child, given birth to his child, loved and raised his child without him.

And all the time he'd been alive.

Alive and so incredibly *vital*.

That really was Nikos in front of her, a wary expression on the face that had lived as nothing but a memory for an agony of time.

The emotions that flooded her were too hot and overwhelming to be contained a moment longer and they overflowed with a howl she had no control over as she leapt at him.

# CHAPTER TWO

NIKOS DIDN'T MOVE away or attempt to defend himself from the fists beating against his chest and the screamed indecipherable words. He kept his composure, his gaze fixed above her head, determined to remain dispassionate against the onslaught of Marisa's rage.

She'd always been his temperamental opposite. Where he was cool and analytical, she was warm and passionate. Even her fury, he was now discovering, was passionately delivered.

But when the impact of her beating fists weakened and he sensed her purge was over, he looked down and his guts twisted.

It wasn't fury that had contorted her beautiful face and turned it into something red and swollen. And it wasn't fury that dropped her to the floor with a thud, made her fall onto her side, pull her knees to her chin and weep in a rocking ball.

Unprepared for such an emotional display, he rubbed his cheek and swallowed air through rapidly tightening lungs.

A box of tissues sat on the suite's bureau and, needing to do something, he strolled over and picked it up then placed it on the floor beside her before finishing his drink.

*Theos*, he needed another one, and poured himself an even heftier measure, which he downed in one. His next measure was more sedate and he poured an equal amount in another glass before taking it to Marisa.

Her sobs and the racking of her frame seemed to be lessening but he kept a cautious distance as he crouched down. 'Here,' he said quietly, speaking in English, a language they were both fluent in. 'Drink this. It will help.'

Marisa wanted to cover her ears and drown out his voice. *Nikos*'s voice. This was simply too much to take in.

All those long nights she had dreamed of this, Nikos alive, the time that had passed since his death nothing but a vivid nightmare.

Oh, God, *he was alive*.

Dragging her trembling hands over her face and trying her hardest to catch a breath in a chest so bruised, she sat up. Not yet ready to look at him again, she took a handful of tissues and blew her nose.

A glass was thrust in front of her face. Fine dark hairs poked out beneath the sleeve of his shirt around his wrist. It was enough to make fresh tears fall and she grabbed more tissues to wipe them away before taking the drink. She threw the liquid down her throat. Unused to neat spirits, she didn't expect the fiery burn that followed but it helped, cutting through the fog of her brain and sharpening her senses.

'Another?' he asked.

Still unable to look at him, she nodded.

When the refilled glass held by the long, tapered fingers appeared before her again, she snatched it off him and downed it.

'Better?'

She blew out a short breath before daring to meet his stare.

He was crouched on his haunches, light brown eyes studying her. 'Ready to talk?'

But her throat was too constricted to speak. Rising to her knees, overwhelmed with the need to touch him and assure herself that she hadn't hallucinated him into life, that Nikos truly was here, mortal, breathing, she reached out a hand and pressed it to his cheek.

Gazing into his intense eyes, she rubbed her thumb over his strong jaw, felt the unshaven dark bristles tickle against it, then gently skimmed it down to his mouth. The heat of his breath warmed her skin before she reached her other hand to his face and traced her fingers over it. The furrowed brow, the lines around his eyes, the long nose that bent a little to the left, the cleft in his chin, not a millimetre of skin left unexplored.

He didn't blink, not even when she brushed her fingers up to the widow's peak of his hairline and dived them through the cropped dark brown hair to trace the contours of his head and down to his neck. Only when she felt the beat of the pulse beneath his ear and felt her own pulse beat in response did she drop her hands and sag back on her bottom.

A beat of charged silence passed before he rose and walked his long, lean frame to the armchair.

Nikos sat heavily and watched Marisa shuffle until her back rested against the base of the sofa opposite him. She hugged her knees to her chest and rested her chin on them.

He tried to gather his thoughts, a task made harder by the sensation dancing over his skin where her fingers had caressed. *Theos*, hers was the first real human touch he'd felt in eighteen months.

Gritting his teeth, he forced himself back to the matter at hand. He'd composed what he would say to her on the flight over, had run over it many times in his head, had known much of the delivery would depend on her reaction to him. He'd guessed emotions would be involved—this was Marisa after all—but he'd never imagined those emotions would be so raw. So hard to witness.

Their affair had lasted much longer than his previous relationships but it had never been serious. Nikos didn't do serious, never had, never would. He liked the bachelor life and greatly disliked being answerable to anyone, a hangover from his teenage years. As he liked to tell people, if you want to watch an innate rebellious streak bloom in real time, send a wilful fourteen-year-old to a strict foreign boarding school.

He'd lasted two terms before being expelled. He'd lasted a whole four months at the next one. He'd only avoided expulsion at the third because his grandfather had bribed him. If Nikos could survive the school year without as much as a sanction *and* pass his exams, he could finish his education and have fifty thousand from his trust fund. There had been other conditions attached but they'd been ignored the minute the money had hit his bank account. He'd been sixteen years old.

Nineteen years later and Nikos still lived his life on *his* terms. Until his forced exile, life had been great. He'd loved making money and he'd loved spending money. He'd loved having the wealth that meant the world's most beautiful women gravitated to him and allowed him to take his pick of the crop.

Marisa had been the first woman he'd actively pursued. She'd been in the VIP section of his Ibiza nightclub when they'd met. Instantly attracted to her, he'd nonetheless assumed she was another vacuous socialite. His assumption that she'd willingly come to his villa for a night of no-strings fun had been swiftly disabused.

Unused to female rejection, he'd gone all out to woo her. She'd agreed to meet him the next day for lunch by the pool at his villa…and had turned up with a gaggle of friends. It had taken a week of messages and calls for her to agree to a date. It had taken another month to get her into bed and then had come the next surprise—she'd been a virgin.

He supposed that's why their affair had lasted as

long as it did. It had been impossible to get bored with someone who refused to play the usual games and constantly kept him on his toes. Marisa had her own life, one she'd been unable and unwilling to revolve around him. Her parents had been grooming her to take over the running of the family shipping business, something she'd taken very seriously.

As he'd had more flexibility with his working hours, Nikos had found himself in the strange realm of being the one to make all the running. It had been worth it. Marisa had taken work seriously but outside office hours she had been excellent company; passionate, funny and witty, open-minded, as happy dining in a cheap café as she was in a Michelin-starred restaurant. That she was as sexy as sin had been the icing on the cake.

She was also naturally affectionate. She would end a short phone call with a good friend saying she loved them. She told *everyone* she loved them. She'd told Nikos she loved him hundreds of times but for Marisa, they were just words, so to have witnessed such naked distress at his resurrection sat heavily in his guts.

He didn't see how it could be real. Even his grandfather hadn't been this emotional at Nikos's return.

He was pretty sure his father hadn't known he'd been missing. Even if he had, Nikos doubted he'd suffered more than a solitary pang. His father hadn't cared for him as a child and cared even less for him as an adult.

Swirling the remaining single malt in his glass

he went straight to the subject that had brought him here. 'You have a son.'

Her brown eyes flickered. He read the surprise in them. He'd often thought how their eyes were mirrors of their personalities; Marisa's dark and warm, his light and cold.

'I saw you with him. Two days ago,' he added when her mouth dropped open.

Tears filled her eyes. He held his breath and warily waited for them to spill over and for her to fall to pieces again.

It didn't happen. She swallowed rapidly and nodded.

'He's mine?'

She brushed a falling tear and nodded again.

He took a large sip of his drink. He'd known it in his heart but having it confirmed still came as a rush.

'You named him for me?' He asked the question though he already knew the answer. He'd seen the birth certificate.

Nikos Marco Lopez. Born eleven months ago weighing three kilograms. Born seven months after he'd faked his own death.

She let go of the hold around her knees and rested her head back against the base of the sofa. 'Why…?' Her husky voice broke.

The sound of her anguish cut straight through him, and he filled the void of silence before she could find her voice again.

'You must have many questions,' he stated. 'Let me explain as best I can. Anything I miss, ask when

I'm finished. And then I will ask questions of you. Fair?'

Her gaze searched his before she closed her eyes and inclined her head in agreement.

He took a moment to put his thoughts in order. 'As you must have guessed, I faked my death. It was not a decision I made lightly. An international drug cartel wanted to use my clubs to sell their goods.' Her already ashen face paled even more and he leaned forward. 'Yes. The same cartel.'

She brought her knees back to her chest.

'They would not accept no as an answer. You remember the firebomb in my London nightclub? That was them. What you don't know is they made a bomb threat against my club in Ibiza. It was fake but I have no doubt they were capable and willing to do it for real. In the space of eight days, my French lawyer, the head of my Santorini security and my club manager in Madrid disappeared. I received a package that contained photos of my missing lawyer. I won't describe them to you but it showed the depraved lengths they were willing to go to in order to force my hand. Among those pictures was a photo of you.'

A whimper came from her tightly compressed lips. He ignored it, just as he ignored the violent churn in his stomach to remember his reaction to finding her photo nestled amid evidence of such cruel barbarity.

'It was clear that no one associated with me would be safe until I gave in. But I would not submit. Drugs are an evil in this world and I will have nothing to do with them.'

Nikos understood too well the inherent wickedness of drugs. His parents had been addicts with the unfortunate blessing of a substantial monthly allowance from a trust fund on his half-English mother's side to feed it. One of his earliest memories was of going into the living room one morning and finding her semi-conscious on the sofa with a needle stuck in her arm.

'I employed an international security firm and with their help, I faked my death and disappeared. My business partners could legally take care of the businesses. My "death" meant the cartel had no reason to go after you or anyone else associated with me.'

There had been no debate in his mind about confiding his plans to Marisa. Safer for her to believe he was dead.

But he couldn't switch off the horror of those photos and for his own peace of mind and to satisfy himself of her safety, he'd employed the same security force to keep watch over her.

'Drowning gave a plausible reason for me to vanish. I was smuggled to Alaska and spent the months of my death alone in a cabin in the Alaska Mountain Range. Without a body, a death certificate can't be issued for a number of years, which meant I could resume my life when it was over.' He raised his shoulders. 'And now it's over.'

Over but with the wreckage still to be cleared.

Despite his best efforts, the Lopezes had still got caught in the cartel's snare. He knew perfectly well it had been incidental to his own dealings with them—the cartel had needed to increase its distribution processes so they could get their evil goods into the nightclubs and other places it was sold—but it had still come as a blow when he'd learned via the daily report he'd received of Marco Lopez's murder a year ago. A devastating blow made harder by being eight thousand kilometres away and helpless to do anything about it.

Marco had been a good man who'd welcomed Nikos into his family, and Nikos's guilt that he'd only had Marisa watched sat like poison in his guts.

That had been the lowest point of his exile. It had also been the moment he'd understood why Felipe Lorenzi, the man who ran the security operation, had insisted on sending him to such a remote part of the world. Sitting idle while the world burned was not Nikos's style but placing him one hundred and twenty kilometres away from the nearest road had gone some way to curbing his impulsive take-charge tendencies.

He didn't like to remember how close he'd come to packing a rucksack and taking his chances in the Alaskan wilderness when he'd learned the devastating news. If Felipe hadn't called to tell him the Lopezes had also hired him to run their personal security in the wake of Marco's death, he would have made that hike.

And if a single one of the daily reports had men-

tioned Marisa's pregnancy or the birth of her child…
*his* child…he dreaded to think what he would have
done.

Marisa tried to process what she'd just been told
but there was so much to wrap her head around. Too
much. Nikos had made a clear and conscious decision to fake his own death. He'd willingly allowed
her to believe he was dead.

She met his stare and hugged her knees tighter.
'Why didn't you tell me?'

He raised a shoulder before having another drink.
'My death had to be convincing. Believable.'

'I understand that… Can I have some more
Scotch?' She would get it for herself but didn't trust
her legs to keep her upright. Everything inside her
felt jellified.

He got to his feet and strolled to the bar. She
couldn't stop herself watching his every move, afraid
that if she took her eyes off him for a second he
would disappear again. None of this felt real.

She clasped the refilled glass tightly while he settled back on the armchair and she tried her hardest to get her scrambled thoughts in order. 'I think
I understand why you did it—faked your death.
That cartel…' she squeezed her eyes shut as memories flashed through her: her father's coffin; gentle
Rocco's dead body floating in the swimming pool
'…were evil. But I don't understand why you didn't
tell me, why you were happy for me to believe you
were dead.'

'I wasn't *happy* about any of it,' he retorted bitingly.

'You could have confided in me. Prepared me. I can keep my mouth shut, especially about something as serious as that.'

'Secrets don't stay secrets if they're shared. And if I had told you, who else should I have told? My grandfather? My business partners?'

His indifference, both in his choice of words and his tone, pummelled through her. When she looked at him and found the indifference there in his stare too, her battered heart withered. 'I would have confided in you,' she whispered.

'You don't know that. Until you're in a situation, you don't know how you would react.'

'There is no way I would have let the man I love think I was dead. I wouldn't have put you through that pain.'

She caught a tiny flinch in his features before he said, 'Not even if you knew the pain would be temporary and that the alternative would mean actual, physical danger?'

Temporary? Marisa had a large sip of the Scotch and let it burn down her throat. 'The cartel was taken down two weeks ago,' she said slowly.

He inclined his head in agreement.

'Why are you only telling me now? Why not then, as soon as the danger was over?'

He took another drink of his own.

'Are you only telling me now because you've learned about Niki?'

His light brown eyes flickered. 'You call him Niki?'

She nodded. She'd named him for his father but the first time she'd said the name aloud she'd burst into tears. It had got easier hearing others say it over time but those tears and the fact that she'd wanted him to have his own identity without the burden of a dead father to live up to had found her developing her own variant of the name.

'What's he like?'

'A baby. He's beautiful. He has your colouring—I think he'll be tall like you too. He's crawling and tries to stand himself up, and he cut his first tooth two weeks ago...' Her words trailed off as she was reminded, again, that Nikos could have safely knocked on her door two weeks ago and put her out of her misery. He'd chosen not to. 'Tell me the truth, Nikos, are you only here now because of Niki?'

'I can't ignore the fact I have a child.'

'No,' she agreed. 'You can't. But what I want to know is would you have told me you were alive if you hadn't found out about him?'

'What would have been the point? You've moved on with your life. You didn't need a ghost from your past showing up.'

She tilted her head back and breathed through the tightening in her chest. 'So that's a no, then.'

'I did what I thought was best.'

'For who? You or me? You can't think I wouldn't have found out eventually. You always intended to resume your life—we have friends in common. Someone would have seen you and told me. Sooner or later the media will pick up on it.' She downed the rest of her Scotch in an effort to drown her growing anger. 'Is that what you wanted for me? To get a call or read an article telling me the man I'd mourned for eighteen months was alive and kicking? Or was it that you didn't care enough to tell me? That rather than it being *me* who'd moved on, it was you and this was one conversation you simply couldn't be bothered to have?'

'I didn't imagine you'd moved on. This is your engagement party.'

'And what, you made assumptions about my state of mind? Stop making excuses and be honest with me. You've had two weeks to tell me you're alive and the only reason you're here telling me now is because of Niki.'

Resting his elbows on his thighs he leaned forward. His features were expressionless as he said the cutting words, 'So what?'

# CHAPTER THREE

MARISA HAD TROUBLE closing her jaw enough to speak. Were her ears deceiving her or had Nikos really just said that? '"*So what*"?'

He shrugged, his expression now nonchalant. 'Yes. So what? We were lovers but you knew the score. I don't do long term and I never pretended differently. I'm not here to resurrect an affair that would have soon died a natural death. You've moved on and I've moved on but that doesn't stop me wanting to know my child and being a father to him.' He swirled the last of the Scotch in his glass and then tipped it down his throat.

Marisa hadn't thought the evening could produce a bigger shock than Nikos being alive but this revelation landed even harder, filling her brain with the dizzying heat that had made her faint only an hour or so before.

It felt like she'd fallen through a trapdoor and had hurtled down and down to land with a thump that left her entire body bruised.

She knew the score? What score? She had a vague

recollection of a date together when they'd talked about dreams for their respective futures and Nikos saying something about never wanting to be tied down, but that had been in their early days, before they'd slept together, before things had intensified so much that being parted had become a physical ache. The nights they couldn't be together had still been spent together, laptops open, catching up on their day and making dirty talk through video calls before wishing each other goodnight.

Did none of that mean anything to him?

And what about all the times she'd told him she loved him? Didn't that mean anything either? He'd never said the words back to her but every time she'd said it, he would either kiss her if they were together in person or blow her a kiss if they were speaking through their laptops or phones.

He was very different from her. She'd known that from the outset. His refusal to say the three magic words would have affected her far more deeply if she hadn't intuited from the little he'd told her of his background that love as a word held no meaning for him. Nikos showed his feelings by deeds and in the six months they'd been together his actions had been those of a man infatuated.

Or was that what she'd wanted to think? Had she seen what she'd wanted to see? Believed what she'd wanted to believe?

She stared into the face that was giving so little away and fought to keep the tears burning the back of her eyes from falling. 'Don't you even care about Raul?'

If Nikos had ever felt anything for her then *surely* he would feel something at her being engaged to another man, and it was taking all the control she had not to fling herself at his feet and beg him to snap out of this horrid ice-cool persona and tell her she wasn't alone in feeling overwhelmed at being in the same room together again, that she wasn't the only one having to control hands that yearned to touch and lips that yearned to caress, an entire body that yearned to wrap around him and feel his warm skin against hers.

The growing desperation for his touch fought with what her eyes were telling her. This icy Nikos was a facet of his personality she'd seen only fleetingly before and never directed at her.

Nikos strove not to let the rancid burn at the mention of Marisa's fiancé show on his face. When he'd learned two months ago during a wet afternoon spent trawling the internet that she'd become engaged, he'd shrugged it off. See? He'd been right that her affection and words of love had been nothing special. She'd picked herself up and found a replacement for him. Good luck to her.

When, later that same night of discovery, he'd found his fingers typing the name of her fiancé into his search engine, he'd been so disturbed at his actions that he'd hurled his phone at the wall. It had been unfortunate that he'd used enough force to crack the screen. His strength had been surprising too, considering how drunk he'd been that night.

He would not accept that his online search of Raul Torres's name earlier that day and all the calls he'd made about him had been like lancing a boil. He'd only done it because her fiancé would be a huge part of his son's life. Any father would do the same.

*Theos*. Him, a father.

'I don't know the man,' he answered evenly, swallowing his anger to stare directly into her eyes. 'But I don't care for what I've heard. Does Nikos think of Raul as his father?'

Her head dropped. She rubbed her hands over her face before answering. 'He hardly knows him and he's too young to think in terms like that.'

'Good.' The relief he felt made his body sag but he ignored it to inject a warning tone into his voice. 'I don't want to make trouble for you, Marisa, but I don't want my son to think of anyone as his father but me.'

But the sickly pallor her skin had turned told him her mind had wandered away from him and his stomach clenched to think it was that man it had wandered to.

'What's wrong?' he asked.

'Where's my handbag?'

'I assume it's where you left it.'

She staggered to her feet. 'My phone's in it. I need to get it.'

'You want to go back to the snake pit for your phone?'

'If there's a problem at home, Estrella won't be able to get hold of me. She's looking after Niki for the night.' Just thinking it was enough for icy shards to stab at Marisa's chest and pierce into her brain. How long had she been uncontactable in this suite?

'She must have your mother and sister's numbers?'

'Yes....'

'Then stop panicking.' He reached into his pocket and pulled out his phone. 'What does your bag look like?'

'Small and silver... Can I borrow that to call Elsa? I know her number by heart.'

He unlocked it and handed it to her. 'If she doesn't answer, we'll call the concierge service. They'll find it.'

Thankfully her sister answered, assured her she was looking after the bag, and promised to bring it to the suite straight away. From the tone of her voice, Marisa could tell she was dying to bombard her with questions but, for once, Elsa restrained herself.

When the call was over, she dragged her feet to the bar where Nikos had moved to, pushed his phone to him, and helped herself to another Scotch.

Marisa had avoided alcohol during the pregnancy and in the weeks she'd unsuccessfully tried to breast-feed, and had barely touched it since. She'd never been a heavy drinker but any tolerance she'd developed would surely have been lost. With the amount of Scotch and the earlier champagne she'd had that night, she should be drunk but the only effect it was having on her was a slight numbing of all the mounting shocks and adrenaline surges.

How could she have forgotten about her phone? It didn't matter that Nikos was right and that the housekeeper could easily get hold of her mother and sister. Niki was her responsibility.

But, dear God, this was all so overwhelming. Impossible. Nikos standing close enough that she could reach out and touch him.

Her grief for him had left her bedbound for weeks. Only the positive pregnancy test had got her out of bed, some maternal instinct kicking in that demanded she take care of herself for the sake of her growing foetus. Her baby had been the spur she'd needed to fight through the despair. His birth and the responsibility that came with it had forced her to nestle Nikos away into the hidden reaches of her heart. Though time had never even begun to heal the pain, it had dulled her memories of how deeply her need for him had consumed her. She'd been like a schoolgirl, daydreaming constantly about him, aching for him, her mind on him wherever she was and whatever she was doing.

To stand beside his towering body now, to watch him breathe, drink, the movements of his mouth and throat when he spoke, the movements of his muscles, flesh and blood, *alive…*

It was too much. Every cell in her body ached to throw itself at him, to rip his black shirt off and press her cheek to his chest and feel the steady beat of his heart in her ear.

And then she caught his baleful stare and nausea roiled in her belly. He wasn't here for *her*. He didn't want her any more. Nikos had moved on in every way imaginable.

Holding her glass tightly, she filled her mouth with the fiery liquid and willed her eyes not to leak again.

He leaned his back against the bar and breathed heavily before saying, 'I meant what I said. I don't want to cause trouble for you, Marisa, but Raul Torres is bad news. From everything I've been told about him, the man's a snake, in business *and* love.'

She swallowed the Scotch and willed even harder for the tears to stay hidden, tried to breathe through the crushing weight in her chest and stomach. 'What business is it of yours?'

Nikos had watched her fall apart at his feet with an indifference that bordered on clinical. He'd just admitted he wouldn't have cared if she'd spent the rest of her life believing he was still dead. He'd never had any intention of seeing her again.

'If you marry him then he has influence over my son,' he said roughly.

'He's not going to have any influence because I'm not marrying him.' She drank more of the Scotch and gave a tiny spurt of near-hysterical laughter. 'It's almost funny. I only went ahead with the party tonight because I didn't want to humiliate him but he's been humiliated in the most public way imaginable. God knows what he'll do now.'

Nikos stared at her. The anger that had pulsed

and churned at the mention of her fiancé reduced fractionally. 'You were already planning to end the engagement?'

'Yes. I thought he was a good choice but I was wrong. He let me believe he'd love Niki as his own but it was a lie. If he cared about Niki he would have been there when we needed help but he abandoned us. It's the business he wants.' She finished her Scotch, placed the glass on the bar and wiped her plump mouth with the back of her hand.

'If he abandoned you,' he said slowly, 'why go ahead with the party? Why care if you humiliate him?'

'Because he's got a vengeful side. He's expecting to take over the running of Lopez Shipping—we were going to align our two businesses. He's already learned too much about how we run ours. He can undermine us and undercut us and steal our contracts and do God knows what other damage. I need to end things amicably. After everything my family's been through these last eighteen months, the last thing I want is another fight.'

'What on earth were you thinking when you agreed to marry him?'

'Actually, he agreed to marry *me*.'

'Marriage was y*our* idea?'

'Yes.'

'What the hell…?' The woman who'd made Nikos do all the running in their relationship had been the one to propose? The notion landed like a white-hot slap.

She spun to face him, eyes narrowed dangerously.

'Have you forgotten that my father was murdered?' she ground out. 'Our dog drowned! Can you imagine what it was like for me to have a newborn baby and a business to run under those circumstances when the cartel was still out there circling my family like sharks? I was juggling a thousand balls on my own and the people who should have helped wouldn't or couldn't.'

'So you went running to Raul Torres?' he accused. 'I learned in one hour of research that he's a snake and you chose *him* as a father to my child?' And a husband for herself.

'I was trying to protect us!'

'You *had* protection!'

'Paid protection! Niki had no father or grandfather. All he had was me and Mama.' She put the bottle of Scotch to her lips but before she could take a swig lowered it again. 'Don't you think that if my son's father hadn't decided to fake his own death without telling me, then things might have been different?' Her face contorted as she swigged the Scotch. 'If you'd confided in me and had the courage to tell me we were over—and, let's be honest, you used the faking of your death as an excuse to dump me without the bother of having to tell me—I would have been hurt but at least I would have known you were out there and that one day you'd come back and be Niki's father. I would have had something to hold onto.'

'Don't blame your lack of judgement on me,' he

snarled. Her insinuation that he'd been too cowardly to end things had hit the intended target.

It was true that he'd had no intention of seeing her again but that was because he'd reasoned they'd had their time together. It would have come to an end anyway. He'd given Marisa more than he'd given any other lover. Given her all he was capable of.

If he'd known there was the smallest chance that she could be pregnant then of course he would have acted differently but he hadn't had the faintest idea and for her to try and put some of the blame for *her* actions on his shoulders was enraging. When he'd made the decision to fake his death, her family had been nowhere near the cartel's radar. He'd never dreamed they could have created a life together either, but he knew it now and he was here, ready to take responsibility and step up to the mark. If he was the coward she implied he'd still be in Mykonos. He would be like his father, happy to leave the burden of an unwanted child on someone else's shoulders. 'I get that it's been a difficult time for you…'

'*Difficult*?' she screamed. 'I gave birth to my son with my father fresh in his grave and thinking the man I loved was fish food!' And with that, she hurled the almost empty bottle of Scotch across the suite. It landed on the dining table and smashed into pieces.

Nikos surveyed the damage, from the shattered mess of glass on and around the table to the woman who was staring at him frozen in white-faced horror.

He was saved from deciding which mess to prioritise by the knock on the door.

Trying to get a grip on the fetid emotions burning his guts, he rubbed the back of his neck. 'That will be your sister.'

'I'll get it.'

He watched her stumble to the door then turned away. He didn't like the way his heart tugged to see her trying to hold her head up, as if she were fighting to regain her dignity.

Swallowing hard in a throat that had inexplicably thickened, he began collecting the larger shards of glass. By the time he'd put them in a bin and called the concierge service to send someone to the suite to clear the rest of it, Marisa and Elsa had finished their murmured conversation and they were alone again.

She stood with her back to the closed door hugging her silver bag to her chest.

'Has Estrella been in touch?' he asked.

'Just to put my mind at ease that Niki's fine.'

'You don't leave him much?' He observed her reaction carefully. Not until he watched Marisa interact with their son would he be able to judge her as a mother but it was necessary to be prepared.

Her shoulders hunched in on themselves as she stepped wearily to the sofa. 'Very rarely.'

She sat heavily and clutched at her head. After a long moment, she met his stare. 'I'm sorry,' she whispered, throat moving and chin wobbling. 'I didn't mean to throw it.'

A spike of guilt sliced through him.

'I'm sorry too. I shouldn't have passed judgement.' And he had no right to feel any kind of jealousy that she'd moved on with her life. It was irrational and no doubt caused by spending eighteen months with only his tortured thoughts for company.

Marisa rubbed her pounding forehead and tried to control the trembles fighting to break out through her.

Since Niki's birth, she'd spent each and every day using all her strength to keep a lid on her emotions. Nikos's return had sprung the lid free and it was terrifying how easily the emotions were taking control of her.

'I know I made a mistake with Raul,' she said, the compulsion to explain too strong to keep contained. 'But, Nikos, I was desperate. All I could think was that Niki deserved a father and that I needed help. My head was all over the place. Grief...' She swallowed and rubbed her forehead even harder, choosing her words carefully. 'I'd lost my father and protector. I didn't want to marry anyone but I thought I needed to, for Niki's sake and for the business's sake.'

'What about for your sake?'

'Those reasons *were* for my sake. I was trying to find some kind of peace of mind. Protecting my son and getting help for the business was the only way for me to have that.'

'Yes, but you can't deny that Raul's a handsome man,' he observed casually. 'Waking up to that face must have made it an easier pill to swallow.'

She clutched her cheeks, immediately understanding his implication. 'God, no, that had no part in it. We didn't… We never…'

His brow rose sceptically. *'Never?'*

*'No!'* Marisa dropped her gaze to the carpet between her feet in a futile attempt to hide the flame of colour scorching her face. 'I wasn't ready.'

She would never have been ready, something Raul, with a ready-made mistress tucked away, had been happy to accept, but there was no way she would admit that to Nikos. Her pride would not allow him to know how desperate her grief for him had been or that the thought of another man touching her left her cold inside, not now that she knew how little she'd meant to him.

To her great relief, their conversation was interrupted by another knock on the door.

This time it was the concierge service. The splinters of glass were vacuumed in short order but the noise was enough to make the pounding in her head feel like a dozen hammers were knocking inside it.

'Headache?' Nikos asked when they were alone again, observing the way she was now clutching her whole head. The colour he hadn't noticed return to her cheeks had drained from her again.

'I don't feel so good.' She didn't sound so good either. Her words had a definite slur to them. 'I think my body's telling me off for all the Scotch…and the champagne.'

'I'll get you some painkillers.'

He found some in his toiletry bag, took a bottle of water from the fridge and handed them to her.

She gave a grateful, wan smile and swallowed the painkillers down with half the water.

'Lie down and rest for a while,' he said.

'I need to speak to Raul.'

'Out of the question.' He wasn't letting her out of his sight.

'Nikos—'

'No,' he cut in firmly. 'You're not in any state to deal with him. Rest, sober up…'

'I'm not drunk.'

'You should be.'

'I know.'

He couldn't help but smile. 'You're not drunk but you *are* feeling the effects. Your body's telling you to rest, so rest. Have my bed if you want.'

She shook her head, the action making her wince. 'I should go home.'

'Is your housekeeper expecting you back?'

'Not until morning.'

'Then rest for a while. I'll get my driver to take us to your home when you're feeling better.'

'Us?'

'I want to see my son, Marisa.' And see with his own eyes what kind of a mother she was. From everything she'd said, he doubted she was as lousy and indifferent a mother as his own had been but he needed to be certain. Words were cheap. If he sensed for a second that she treated their son as an encumbrance or neglected him in any way, he would sue for custody. He hoped it wouldn't come to that.

'Okay,' Marisa whispered, resting her head back.

Her head was *killing* her. 'You can see him but you'll have to wait until morning to meet him properly. He's grouchy like his father when he doesn't get enough sleep.'

Nikos's faint chuckle was the last thing she remembered before she fell asleep.

## CHAPTER FOUR

NIKOS, ARMS FOLDED across his chest, gazed at Marisa
fast asleep on the sofa in exactly the same position
she'd been when he'd left the suite an hour ago. He
should wake her. That couldn't be a comfortable position to sleep in.

He whispered her name. No response.

Swallowing back the lump in his throat, he placed
a finger to her shoulder and carefully prodded. No
response.

He stepped back and considered his options. He
could leave her as she was or carry her to his bed.
When he'd lifted her into his arms earlier after her
faint it had been an automatic reaction, something
he'd done without any forethought.

A small part of him acknowledged he'd swept her
out of the party room before Raul regained his wits
enough to try and bring her round himself.

He could hardly believe the rush of exultation that
had swept through him at Marisa's admission that
she hadn't slept with her fiancé.

Marisa was the only woman Nikos had been with

whose sexual appetite matched his own. His shock at her virginity had quickly been forgotten as her inhibitions had disappeared. In the bedroom, she'd blossomed, gained a voracious appetite that had blown his mind and fed his own hunger into a heady lust that had kept him with her far longer than he usually stayed with a lover. As bad as it had been to imagine her enjoying those same heady, sensual appetites with that vile man, he wouldn't have thought any less of her for it. Humans were carnal creatures, Marisa especially so.

What had stopped her enjoying them with Raul? Did motherhood reduce a woman's libido?

He took another step back and cursed himself for speculating and exulting over something that was none of his business. It was natural that he would still feel stirrings for her. There hadn't been anyone since her, no one for him to transfer his lust to. He would rectify that as soon as possible.

Spinning on his heel, he strode to the suite's bedroom and looked in the wardrobe. There, he found spare bedding. He grabbed some and carried it back to the living area.

Working swiftly, he put the pillow on the edge of the sofa and then gently coaxed her flat so her head rested on it.

She stirred and mumbled something that made him freeze and sent his pulses soaring.

It sounded like she'd said his name.

For a passage of time that lasted an age, he stared

at her beautiful face, hardly able to breathe, the thuds of his heart echoing in his ears.

She stirred again and pulled her knees up to the foetal position. The familiarity of it wrenched something in his chest.

He gritted his teeth and forced air into his lungs.

It was late. It had been a far more emotional evening than he'd anticipated and he too had drunk more Scotch than was good for him. It was no wonder his reactions were all over the place. A few hours' sleep would put him back on his usual even keel.

In one burst of action, he pulled her shoes off, draped the blanket over her and strode to the suite's bedroom, closing the door behind him.

Marisa opened her eyes, going from heavy sleep to full alertness in an instant.

*Nikos.*

He was alive.

Or had she dreamt it?

A look at her watch told her it was four in the morning.

She threw the soft blanket off—where had that come from? Had he put it on her?—and her stockinged feet sank into thick carpet.

Rubbing her eyes, she stared at the sofa. At some point while she'd slept, Nikos had put a pillow under her head, laid her flat on her side and covered her.

She hadn't dreamt him.

Heart in her throat, she found herself in the adjoining room before she even knew she'd opened the door and walked into it.

The light in there was incredibly faint, the little illumination coming from the lamp Nikos had left on for her in the living area. It was enough for her to see the shape of his body nestled under the covers, breathing deeply.

She definitely hadn't dreamt him.

Nikos was alive.

The relief was almost as overwhelming as it had been the first time, and, eyes glued to his sleeping shadowed face, she stretched out a trembling hand and lightly pressed her fingers against his cheek. The warmth of his skin made her sag with fresh relief and assailed her with memories of the joy she'd felt to wrap herself against him at night and bask in the heat that had radiated from his body. After their first night together, any nights spent alone had always felt so cold. From the nightmare day she'd been told he was missing, the coldness had lived in her constantly.

The relief was short-lived. A hand twice the size of her own flew like a rocket from under the sheet and wrapped around hers.

'What are you doing?'

Her heart jumped into her throat, the beats vibrating through her suddenly frozen body.

Nikos raised his head and blinked the sleep from his eyes, trying to clear the thickness from his just awoken brain, and stared at the motionless form standing beside him.

'Marisa?' His voice sounded thick to his own ears too. Was he really awake? Or dreaming?

As his eyes adjusted he saw the shock in her wide eyes before his gaze drifted down to notice the buttons of her dress around her bust had popped open in her sleep to show the swell of her breast in the black lace bra she wore.

Arousal coiled its seductive way through his bloodstream to remember the taste of her skin on his tongue and the heady scent of her musk. He tugged her closer to him, suddenly filled with the need to taste it again, taste *her* again, to hear the throaty moans of her pleasure and feel the burn of their flesh pressed together. It was a burn he'd never felt with anyone but her.

Her lips parted. Her breath hitched. Her face lowered to his…

His mouth filled with moisture, lips tingling with anticipation. He put his other hand to her neck and his arousal accelerated.

It had been so long…

Then, with her mouth hovering just inches from his, she jerked back and snatched her hand away. It fluttered to her rising chest.

'I'm sorry for waking you,' she whispered, backing away some more. 'I was just checking I hadn't dreamt you.'

And then she disappeared from his room as silently as she'd entered it, leaving him blinking at the empty space she'd filled only seconds before.

Nikos put his fingers to his cheek. If he couldn't

still feel the burn from the mark of her touch, he would believe he'd just dreamt the whole thing.

Marisa unlocked the door and stepped inside the reception room. She removed her shoes and waited for Nikos to do likewise. In silence, they headed for the stairs. It was only six thirty. She'd messaged Estrella to tell her she was coming home. Her mother would still be in the suite she'd expected to share with Marisa at the hotel but the rest of household would be sleeping. There was one member of it, though, that she was confident would be awake. Her son.

The silence between her and Nikos had been almost total since he'd appeared in the suite's living area, freshly showered and ready to meet his son.

Neither of them had mentioned her visit to his bedroom. If she had her way it would never be spoken of. It had been a foolish, impulsive thing to do. She tried not to beat herself up about it but it was hard. It seemed like everything she did lately was wrong.

But when she opened her son's bedroom door and found him lying on his back, kicking his plump legs in the air, she allowed herself the credit of knowing that when it came to him, she mostly got things right. He was a happy, healthy baby. What mother could ask for more?

As soon as he saw her, his legs kicked even more frantically and he held his arms out to her.

She leaned over to scoop him up. 'Good morning, baby boy,' she murmured, kissing his cheek.

Wide awake, he grabbed at her hair and jiggled in her arms. And then he caught sight of the stranger in the midst and stared at his father with frank curiosity.

Nikos found himself holding his breath, his stare totally and utterly captivated by the chunky bundle in Marisa's arms. Eyes of a colour he couldn't determine were fixed on him, cute little mouth making funny blowing noises. He had a cleft in his chin Nikos recognised from his own baby photos.

His heart swelled. For a moment he felt lightheaded.

That was his son.

He blinked and caught Marisa's cautious stare.

'Do you want to hold him?' she asked.

He'd never held a baby in his life. 'How breakable is he?'

'If you don't drop him, we won't find out.' Then she smiled. 'You won't drop him, so don't worry. Here.' She passed the happy, curious child to him.

Baby Nikos, completely unperturbed to be handed to a stranger, immediately grabbed at Nikos's nose.

Having expected something light and noticeably fragile, it was a relief to feel his son's solidity, even if it did come with additional bounce.

He laughed and met Marisa's stare again. 'He's *beautiful*,' he said, awestruck.

'Yes. He is.' She sighed but her expression was as enchanted as he knew his must be. It was an expression that put to rest his fears that she could be anything like his own mother. Then her expression changed into something wistful. 'Let me change his nappy and then we'll get him some breakfast.'

The hours that passed were the most surreal of Nikos's life. As someone who'd never wanted to be tied down by anything so had never considered having a child, even as some distant future thing, the depth of feelings for his son were like nothing he'd felt before. And they were immediate. One look and he'd been spellbound.

But that wasn't the most surreal aspect. Marisa's willingness to show him the ropes and to answer all his questions about their child—and there were many, he had almost a year of his son's life to catch up on—was astounding. Considering how his resurrection had affected her, he'd braced himself for a fight, had half expected her to make a quick introduction and then boot him out of her home.

He'd also braced himself for her mother's appearance but Rosaria had surprised him too. She'd returned from the hotel and joined them for brunch in the dining room, much thinner than he remembered but as impeccably made up, her demeanour curious but with only a little of the frostiness he'd expected.

Not until Marisa announced she was going to put their son down for a nap and would take a shower, leaving him and Rosaria alone together, did she bring up the elephant in the room. Namely, his faked death.

He explained it as he'd done to Marisa the night before. She listened carefully and asked many questions, only little tells of emotions flickering on her face. He'd just finished his narration when Marisa returned.

When she'd left the dining room she'd still been wearing the ugly party dress she'd slept in and her hair had turned into something that had resembled a rat's nest.

The transformation was remarkable. Her slim body was wrapped in a summery patterned teal chiffon off-the-shoulder dress that fell just below the knees, her hair damp and already drying into its natural curl with no frizz in sight. She'd applied a little make-up and, as she strode to the table, he found himself straightening when he caught a waft of her perfume. She smelled amazing.

She sat next to her mother opposite him and poured herself a coffee before turning her dark brown stare on him. 'You've been filling Mama in on your death?'

Nerve endings stirring, he clenched his hands and shifted in his seat as he inclined his head. 'Is Niki sleeping?' Nikos couldn't believe how easily the diminutive of his son's name had come to him.

'Yes.' She put the baby monitor on the table.

'Good. I have a proposition to discuss with you both.'

His lips twitched to see their heads tilt in unison.

'I want to buy into your business.'

The time spent alone after putting Niki down for his nap had given Marisa time to collect herself. She'd been certain Nikos would want to discuss access and custody and all the things he, as a father, had a right to discuss, and she had wanted to be cool, calm and collected enough to deal with it.

The traumas of the last eighteen months had aged her inside and out. She'd carried a child. Her previously flat stomach was now rounded with silvery scars across her abdomen. Permanent exhaustion meant her skin no longer glowed with health and vitality, but the simple acts of showering and changing into non-horrible clothes had calmed her and made her feel better in herself, and she'd entered the room confident she was now in the right mental space to handle him.

But her confidence had been a delusion. One look at Nikos breathing and talking was enough to make her poise wobble. His comment that he wanted to buy into the business shattered it.

Nikos's stare flickered to her mother before his light brown eyes settled on her. 'If you're in agreement, we'll have the business independently audited and I will pay the recommended value for a third share of it. We will draft an agreement where the three of us each own a third or, if you prefer, the two of you and Elsa own two-thirds between you. Marisa retains overall control but we appoint someone—I have someone in mind—to manage the day-to-day running of it.' He nodded his head at her. 'That person will report directly to you.'

Marisa was too dumbfounded to speak. Nikos owned a chain of nightclubs across Europe. He invested in tech companies. His business interests were diverse but the common theme amongst them was that they were 'hip'. The Lopezes' shipping company was far too old-school and traditional to ever be called hip. In their six months together he'd been interested in the work she did but had never shown the slightest interest in the business as an entity, so for him to make this proposition...

It was left to her mother to pull herself together and ask the pertinent question. 'You want to buy into the business...but *why*?'

'To dissuade Raul Torres from starting a war against you.' He turned his gaze back to Marisa. 'I spoke to him last night, after you fell asleep. You were right about him wanting revenge for ending your engagement.'

Her head felt light. Fuzzy. Since waking, she'd been so wrapped up in Nikos and their son that she'd forgotten all about Raul. 'You spoke to him? About our engagement?' While she'd been zonked out on his sofa?

He shrugged. 'He called your phone. I didn't want to wake you so I answered it. We met in the lobby.'

Marisa clutched at her cheeks, digging her nails into the skin to sharpen her wits. 'What did you talk about?'

'It wasn't a long conversation. I told him the engagement was off and that your businesses would no longer be aligning. He wants the ring returned,' he added indifferently.

She touched the finger it should have been on. She'd stopped wearing the ring within weeks of the engagement, only slipping it on when she saw Raul. It had never felt right there.

It had been little over half a day since Nikos had appeared like a ghost at her engagement party. He'd lobbed one shock after another at her, all without breaking a sweat. Look at him now, announcing the termination of her engagement and the business deal she'd arranged with the nonchalance of someone announcing what they'd be having for their dinner.

She inhaled deeply through her nose and said through gritted teeth, 'What gave you the right to do that?'

'Can someone tell me what's going on?' her mother interjected. 'You're ending your engagement to Raul?'

Glaring at Nikos for revealing something she hadn't got round to telling her mother about, she braced herself. 'Yes.'

'Thank God for that.'

Marisa faced her mother, open-mouthed with shock.

Her mother smiled wanly and shrugged. 'I never thought he was right for you.'

'Then why didn't you say anything?'

'I did try,' she reminded her gently, her eyes conveying a reminder of a conversation between them that she would never repeat in front of Nikos. That she'd thought it was too soon for her. That Marisa shouldn't commit to another man when her heart still belonged to Nikos.

Marisa had batted her mother's doubts away. Giving her heart wasn't part of the deal with Raul. She had no choice when it came to loving her son, that was something primal and ferocious, but her love for Nikos had been too strong, the pain of his loss too much to ever risk feeling like that about anyone again.

Turning back to Nikos, she glared at him even as her heart cried. 'I want you to explain why you took it on yourself to end my engagement when I have a voice of my own.'

Her eighteen months spent mourning him had allowed her to put rose-tinted glasses on some of the less savoury aspects of his personality, namely his take-charge attitude. She wouldn't go so far as to call him a control freak but when given a problem, he would immediately see a solution and implement it, which was great if you'd asked for a solution, not so great if you hadn't.

She remembered them speaking via their personal laptops once when her screen had kept turning itself off. In the morning, a package had arrived before she'd set off for work. A brand new laptop from Nikos. It hadn't occurred to him that she would prefer to fix her current laptop and that if it wasn't fixable, choose a new one for herself. She'd been touched at the gesture but irritated that he'd gone ahead and sorted it without any consultation with her.

'You were worried he'd turn nasty,' he said with a shrug. 'And you were right to be. But he will only pick a fight he knows he can win. He'll think twice about starting a war against you if I'm part of the business.'

Her jaw would snap if she ground her teeth any harder. 'Is that because only a man can save us?'

His eyes flashed. 'No, because I'm someone who's dealt with bullies like him before and know how to handle them.'

'What do you think we've spent the past year doing against the cartel?' she snapped back. 'My mother met with their representatives *on her own* with a secret recording device to get evidence against them. Hers was the only non-circumstantial evidence that allowed their arrests. Without her *you'd* still be playing dead.'

Nikos dug the tips of his fingers on the table and leaned forward, glowering into the furious wide brown eyes.

He knew exactly the danger Rosaria had put herself in, knew too that she'd done it out of the protective mothering instinct his own mother had been born without. The united front and open defiance the whole Lopez family, Marisa included, had shown the cartel in the face of their intimidation tactics and violence had been astounding, but her insinuation that he'd hidden away like a coward until it was all over was beyond insulting.

That it was also close to how he'd felt during those impossibly long months only added fuel to his fury.

Having to stay hidden, far from civilisation, thousands of kilometres from the action, reliant on emailed reports for news of what the hell was going on, unable to influence *anything*, his only contribution the millions of his own money he'd thrown into it, had been torture. If the cabin he'd been given to bunker down in hadn't needed constant maintenance, he would have gone stir crazy.

He'd given up his life to bring those bastards down. He'd lived as a recluse in an alien landscape. He'd done all that in part to protect *her*. To neutralise the cartel's interest in her as a means to get to *him*.

'What you two did to help defeat the cartel was incredible,' he said, keeping a tight hold on his anger. 'But Raul is a different kind of danger. You said so yourself. During my talk with him last night, I made it clear that if he attempts any kind of sabotage, I'll come after him.'

Mimicking his pose, she put her own fingers on the table and leaned towards him. 'For all we know, your threats might have made it more likely that he'll try to sabotage us.'

'My buying into the company puts my presence front and centre for him, and if he's got any sense and searches my history, he'll learn I'm not a man who makes threats—I make promises.' There was a big part of him that hoped Raul *did* try some sabotage. It would give him the excuse he needed to destroy the man who'd abandoned his son and his son's mother when they'd most needed him.

Never had he felt such loathing for another human being, different even from his hatred for the cartel who'd wreaked such evil damage. Every second of their chat had been spent fighting the urge to ram his fist in his face. Not even spelling out in graphic detail exactly what he would do should Raul attempt any retribution against the Lopezes and witnessing the Spaniard's smug exterior crack had sated the urge.

'You didn't even consult me about it!' she raged. 'You took it on yourself to end my engagement and threaten, promise, whatever you want to call it, a man I categorically told you I did *not* want to start a war with!'

'My chat with him last night was to prevent a war,' he bit back.

Her dark brown eyes were ablaze and locked on his, the sparks shooting from them landing on his skin and penetrating into his bloodstream. The angry colour heightening her cheeks brought to mind so clearly the exact shade on her skin when he brought her to orgasm that he pressed his fingers even harder on the table to stop them snatching her to him. *Theos*, she aroused him, every part of him.

'And I don't know why you're directing your anger at me when I'm trying to help you,' he continued. 'You proposed to Raul because you wanted a father for Niki and help in running the business—*I'm* his father and I'm offering you that help. I'm also offering an investment in it and giving you the opportunity that *you* wanted to have someone help you so you can take a step back without losing control. My offer gives you everything you wanted with added protection *and* your family retains majority control.'

The babbling that suddenly came through the baby monitor cut through the tense atmosphere like a grenade.

# CHAPTER FIVE

Marisa looked from the baby monitor to Nikos, blinking rapidly as she got to her feet. 'I'll get him,' she said tightly. 'Mama, don't agree to anything without me.'

Her exit did nothing to lessen the tension permeating the air, which had tautened Nikos's muscles.

Rosaria had dropped her attempt at friendliness, her demeanour now cool and scrutinising. She studied him for a long time before speaking. 'Why do you really want to buy into our business?'

'For the reasons I've already said. Your family has been through enough—it doesn't need a war with Raul Torres.'

'I was never happy about that relationship. There's something about him I never trusted. I offered to stay on and help her with the business but my role was so limited there was little help I could give.' Her tone softened, eyes turning misty. 'Marisa inherited her business brain from her father.'

The business had always been her father's domain, Nikos remembered. Rosaria had been involved too but to a much lesser extent. Both Marco and Rosaria had looked forward to handing the reins to Marisa and retiring together. And Marisa had looked forward to it too. He'd admired her dedication, her insistence in learning every single aspect of the business before she took over, her determination to run it as well and as profitably as her father had.

It was supposed to happen when she turned twenty-five. She'd turned that age two months ago. The business had been hers a year before she would have considered herself ready to take it on.

Suddenly it hit him fully what a torrid time she'd had. The responsibility that had been cast onto her young shoulders. All that while grieving, juggling the threat of the cartel and the demands of a new-born baby.

The angry tension in his muscles loosened as he imagined the strength it must have taken her to get through all that.

'But Marisa is headstrong,' Rosaria continued in a stronger voice. 'You tell her not to do something, she's twice as likely to do it. She inherited that from me. But what I don't understand is why *you* would want to help us in this way.'

'For my son. Taking the pressure off Marisa can only benefit him, and I'm not being entirely altruistic—it's a good investment.'

'I know it's a good investment.' Her gaze did not waver. 'What I'm wondering is if your intention is to invest in my daughter too.'

*Invest in a bed to take her in*, he thought before he

could stop himself. His blood still hummed from the fire that had blazed between them only minutes ago.

*Theos*, he needed to find himself a new lover.

Keeping his tone even, he said, 'My only interest in your daughter now is as the mother of my son.'

Rosaria leaned across the table and covered his hand, forcing him to keep their stares locked together. 'Marisa has been to hell. If you ever had any feelings for her, do not put her back there. And don't look at me like that,' she continued when he raised a brow. 'Marisa is as strong a woman as I've ever known but she's only human. I won't have her hurt again. If you don't see yourself having a future with her then…'

'I've already made that clear to her,' he interrupted, removing his hand. Then, reminding himself that this was a woman whose husband had been killed and whose youngest daughter had been targeted for kidnap, he modulated his tone. 'I'm not here to rekindle our old relationship. We've both moved on but we do need to form an amicable relationship for our son's sake.' He knew better than anyone how children could suffer from parents at war who put their own needs and desires first.

'You don't need to worry about me, Mama. Nikos and I are history.'

The buzz in his veins flared up again.

Carrying their son in her arms, Marisa strode back to her seat. She threw a saccharine sweet smile at him before speaking to her mother. 'Tell me you haven't agreed to anything yet.'

'I'm going to respect your judgement on this one,' her mother said before slipping into Spanish. 'If you do agree to it, make sure you have it written into any contract that he's forbidden from killing himself again.'

Marisa's gaze landed on him as she replied, also in Spanish, 'I'd kill him myself if he did that again.'

A surprising bubble of mirth rose up his throat, a welcome antidote to the bile that had lodged in it at Marisa's chirpily delivered announcement that they were history.

Shouldn't he be relieved that she considered them over, the same way he did?

When he'd faked his death it had been with the full knowledge that the fake termination of his life was the real termination of his relationship. His gallows humour had made him wryly acknowledge that at least he wouldn't have to deal with the histrionics that always came with ending a relationship, even those that had lasted only a fraction of the time spent with Marisa.

When Rosaria left the room and they were left alone with their son, Marisa's eyes narrowed. 'Did you understand that?'

'Yes.'

'Since when do you speak my language?'

'Boredom's a killer when you're dead,' he quipped to counteract the needles prickling over his skin to remember the endless, lonely evenings spent listening to online Spanish tutorials. He'd figured that seeing as he had hours of time on his hands, he might as well use it productively. He would listen to it in bed too, drifting into sleep with the rhythm of the Spanish language playing like music into his ears.

'You taught yourself?' If she was impressed, she was doing an excellent job of hiding it.

'I now understand it perfectly. It's speaking it I need practice with.'

'Then you'll soon get plenty of practice—the majority of our staff speak only a little English and I doubt any of them speak Greek.'

His pulse quickened and he leaned forward. 'Does that mean you accept my proposal?'

She studied him in the same impervious manner her mother had done only minutes before. 'With conditions.'

He was the one doing her a favour. His offer was more than generous. And she had the nerve to impose conditions on him?

He'd forgotten how magnificent she could be.

'Name them.'


Marisa peered closely into the mirror to check her make-up hadn't smudged, then added more lip gloss. She'd always taken pride in her appearance—her deliberate attempt to sabotage her own engagement notwithstanding—but there were occasions when it mattered more than others and seeing Nikos came into that category. Her pride wouldn't let him see her at anything less than her best. She needed all the confidence she could muster to handle being in the same room as him.

In the two weeks since his return from the dead, she'd had to dress and present herself at her best every single day because Nikos was always around, visiting Niki every evening and dining with them as a family. Then there had been the numerous visits to the business headquarters and the docks and the many meetings with their respective lawyers to thrash out their business agreement. She literally couldn't get rid of him. He gave every impression of someone planning to hang around Valencia for the rest of his life.

But he wasn't hanging around Valencia for her. He was hanging around for their son. If not for Niki, she still might not yet know that Nikos was alive. He wouldn't have cared if she'd learned about his resurrection by social media or through her social circle's grapevine.

He wasn't worth an ounce of the pain he'd put her through.

She never dropped her guard around him and worked religiously to maintain a serene if aloof front. She made sure to always keep her tone amiable and whenever their hands brushed when passing their son between them, she gave no reaction at all. Most importantly, she made sure not to stare at him. The times their eyes locked she would deliberately unfocus hers, so as not to feel the effect of his.

When they'd been together she'd seen what she'd wanted to see. Now she only let him see what she wanted him to see because if he could see the truth, he'd see she was holding on by her fingertips.

This was the man she'd been besotted with, the man whose death had come close to breaking her. To get through the days of her grief without him, she'd had to nestle her love and pain deep in her heart. Now, to get through the days with him, she had to bury those old feelings and never, ever let them out. Let emptiness swathe her and replace the fear and pain.

It was the hardest fight of her life.

There was a light knock on her bedroom door before her mother appeared. 'Are you ready?'

Marisa took a deep breath and nodded.

Rosaria stood behind her and together they stared at their reflections.

'I'm proud of you, darling.' Her mother captured one of Marisa's curls in her fingers. 'Your father would be too.'

She closed her eyes and willed back the burn of tears. It was because of her father that she'd agreed to Nikos's business proposition. The contracts cementing the deal would be signed in an hour.

How badly she'd wanted to throw his offer back in his face, but that would have been her pride talking and acting for her.

Her father had inherited the shipping business from his own father and had taken such pride in running it to the same high standards that Marisa had always wanted to do the same for him. He'd worked his backside off to give his family a good life and his daughters the best education money could buy and had still managed to be a wonderful, present father *and* taken their dead housekeeper's orphaned son under his wing and mentored him from a screwed-up rebellious teenager into a billionaire businessman.

Nikos's deal meant her family's legacy would live on and all the pressure she'd been under would be lifted. The structures they were putting in place for the business meant she could take a back seat for as long as she wanted and devote her time and attention solely to her son.

Best of all, her son had a father. Not just *a* father but *his* father, and Nikos was proving himself an attentive and loving one. Everything she'd wanted her son to have.

She would just have to learn to live her life with the man she'd once imagined her future with, as a part of her future. But not for her sake. Loving her son but not loving her.

'Come on,' she said, taking her mother's hand and squeezing it. 'Let's get this done.'

'Have you decided what you're having?' Nikos asked. Marisa's face had been hidden behind the leather-bound lunch menu ever since they'd been shown to their table, dropping it only to thank the waiter for her glass of wine.

She lowered it an inch for her eyes to peer over. 'I think so.'

He nodded at the hovering waiter, who was at their table in a flash, and gave his order.

Marisa's face appeared in its entirety and she followed suit.

'See,' he teased when they were alone again and she didn't have a menu to hide behind any more. 'That wasn't so hard.'

'I was trying to decide what to eat.' She sipped at her wine, eyes flickering from him to the artwork on the restaurant's walls. It was something she often did, a subtle refusal to engage with him unless it was about their son or the business. Infuriatingly, her behaviour only made him want to engage with her more, to provoke a reaction, to feel the weight of those large brown eyes on him as she hung on his every word.

He knew this was contrary to everything he'd told her *and* himself because, doubly infuriating, he was constantly having to clamp down on the thickening of his blood and loins whenever she was within fifty feet of him and having to stop himself goading her into arguments just for the pleasure of seeing her cheeks saturate with colour and her eyes blaze with the passion that always roused him.

He wanted to goad her now, tear her attention from the abstract painting she was studying and force her attention on *him*. He supposed it was like when a child was denied something—it only made them want it more.

Other than that first night when she'd fallen apart and couldn't tear her eyes from his face, Marisa acted not only as if the previous eighteen months hadn't happened but as if their time together had never happened either. She accepted him as part of their son's life while carefully keeping herself at arm's length.

It had become obvious that though she'd behaved rashly in her proposal to Raul, she really had moved on with her life without Nikos. Whatever pain his 'death' had caused her had been fleeting. Her reaction to his return had been nothing more than a large dose of shock, and he'd come to the conclusion Rosaria's warning about not hurting Marisa were the words of an overprotective mother.

In the two weeks he'd spent in Valencia, he'd learned Marisa was as overprotective of their son as Rosaria was of her. Marisa rarely let Nikos out of her sight, her home office more of a crèche than a place of work.

She was still studying that damned painting. How could it hold her interest so thoroughly? It looked like something a child would paint.

'Can we talk business?' he asked, and instantly regretted his rough tone. Not only was he thinking like a child denied attention but now he was acting like one.

Strangely, as a child, he'd never acted in such a way. He'd learned at too young an age that begging for attention only provoked greater indifference. Only when he'd been taken into his grandfather's custody and given a window into how other families lived had he started to understand their neglect and to ask questions.

The biggest question had been what was so damn wrong with him that his parents couldn't love him and had willingly given him up?

Marisa's large brown eyes locked on his, her expression open, almost serene. 'What's on your mind?'

How infuriating that he should be frustrated by *her* indifference.

It just proved he'd been right all along that whatever feelings she'd once had for him had been fleeting. Unsustainable.

But her love for their son was neither fleeting nor unsustainable. She would never give Niki up like Nikos's parents had given him up.

A chill ran up his spine.

What if one day she were to look at Nikos and see what his parents had seen? What if she saw in him whatever it was they'd seen and decided Niki was better kept from him?

He took a sharp breath to counter the disquiet racing through him and curved his mouth into a cool smile.

That scenario would never happen. He would never allow it.

'I brought you here to celebrate so let's celebrate.' He raised his wine glass. 'To a successful business collaboration.'

She clinked hers to it. 'I'll drink to that.'

He drank and raised his glass again. 'And to the successful end of your engagement.'

Her eyes narrowed but she clinked her glass to his. 'Let's hope there aren't any consequences.'

'If there are, he'll pay for them. I'll see to it personally. The business will be protected.'

'I'm counting on it. It's the only reason I agreed to

your buy-in. *Salud*.' She tilted half her wine into her mouth. The act was neither salacious nor provocative but the awareness that always thrummed under his skin when he was with her intensified.

Marisa looked at the giant langoustines placed before her and laughed. It sounded natural, she was sure of it.

This celebratory meal was the first time they'd been alone together since Nikos's return and she found herself working twice as hard to maintain a cool front and fight her eyes desire to fall onto his gorgeous face. She had to avoid too much eye contact with him. She'd become lost in his light brown gaze too many times before.

'If the main course is as big as the starters, I'll have to tell Santi not to cook too much for us tonight,' she said lightly.

'You're going to your sister's?'

'She wants to show off Santi's cooking. I meant to tell you earlier. Don't worry, you're invited.'

'That's good of them to include me but I'm flying to Ibiza later.'

At this, her heart juddered and her composure cracked. Her hand spasmed against her wine glass, sending the pale liquid flying.

Cheeks flaming instantly, she was saved from the weight of Nikos's suddenly piercing stare by a passing waiter hurrying to clean it up and refill her glass.

Nikos was leaving? That should be something to celebrate, not something that made her chest feel like icy shards were penetrating it.

'It's not like you to be clumsy,' he commented when they were left alone again, thoughtful eyes fixed on hers, forehead indented with the contemplative lines she recognised.

'It was an accident.' She tried to speak dismissively but there was a tremor in her voice. Her bones felt like they'd become jellified again.

His right eyebrow rose sardonically.

She had a large drink of her fresh wine and willed her heart to settle.

'What are you going to Ibiza for?' she asked, and was relieved that this time her voice had mostly returned to the casual tone she'd spent two weeks perfecting.

There was a slight narrowing of his light brown eyes before they glittered and a knowing smile played on his lips. 'I need to check in with the club.' A flash of white teeth. 'Let them see in person that I'm not dead.'

'Do your staff know?'

Nikos put a scallop in his mouth and nodded slowly, not taking his eyes from her beautiful face.

Marisa's reaction to the news about him leaving had his heart pumping hard with triumph.

In one beat of a moment, the self-possessed, collected woman who'd treated him with an almost brittle cordiality had lost control. Just one brief second, enough to be a clumsy insignificance were it not for the effects of it still showing, there in the flush of her cheeks, in the quiver in her voice, in the unsteadiness of her hands.

When he'd swallowed the scallop, he said, 'Everyone who needs to be notified has been but it's time for me to show my face again and see for myself that everything's running as it should be in all the various clubs and businesses. It's something I'd planned to do before but learning about our son and sorting out everything with your business changed that.'

A host of emotions played on the face he could see straining not to give anything else away. 'I imagine it will take you a while to get through them.'

He added more food to his fork. 'My PA has arranged for me to visit them and sit down with each management team over a week.'

'Sounds like you're going to be busy.'

'It will be non-stop. It should have been spread over two weeks but I wanted it condensed to get it done as quickly as possible.' Limiting the time he had to spend apart from his son.

'Will we see you in that time?' she asked with a casualness that would have been convincing if her cheeks weren't still flaming and her eyes darting everywhere but at him.

'I hope to make a couple of visits back to Valencia when time allows… If that's agreeable to you?'

'Of course,' she said brightly. 'Niki's become very attached to you.'

*What about his mother?* he wondered idly. 'And I've become very attached to him too.'

'I had noticed,' she said with a dry nonchalance that might have passed as natural if he wasn't watching her so closely.

'And it's with that attachment in mind that I have a request to make of you.'

Having just popped some more langoustine into her mouth, she arched an eyebrow in query.

He leaned forward. 'When I have finished checking in with all my management teams, I want to take Niki home.'

The colour drained from her face and the fork in her hand dropped onto her plate. Her eyes widened and her shoulders hunched as she placed a hand to her chest. She cleared her throat. 'You want to take him to Mykonos?'

'And you,' he clarified.

'Me?' The sudden dread that had clutched Marisa vanished under the surge of her racing pulse and she found herself arching towards him. 'You want me to come too?'

His speculative stare held hers. 'He's still getting to know me and he's too young to leave you yet.'

The brief rush of adrenaline flatlined. She didn't even know why she'd experienced it. This was the man who'd faked his own death with no thought or concern about her and, even if she could forgive that—not his reasons for faking his death which she understood, but his complete dismissal of her in his planning and execution of it—she couldn't forgive or forget his failure to let her know he was alive once it was all over. If he hadn't spotted Niki, he'd have been happy never seeing her again. She meant nothing to him. He didn't want her. She was welcome in his home only as the mother of his son.

Well, she didn't want him either. He was welcome in her home only as the father of her son. If he got down on his knees and begged for them to start over, she would laugh in his face.

She just wished she didn't wake every morning with panic in her heart that she'd dreamt his resurrection and that every minute spent with him didn't make her feel so jittery and flushed inside. It was there now, the heat that had lived in her the entire time they'd been together, the cells of her body straining towards him, her pulse never settling into a steady rhythm.

'Let our son visit my home, *agapi mou*,' he said, light brown eyes boring into her. 'My heritage is his heritage. He deserves to know about it, do you not agree? And one day, everything I have will be his.'

Her cheeks flamed at the endearment that had slipped off his tongue so smoothly she was sure he hadn't noticed. 'When you put it like that, how can I say no?'

She couldn't. She knew that. Not unless she wanted to be actively cruel.

It astounded her how quickly the bond between father and son had formed but it was there and it was real and it was a *good* thing. All children deserved to have the best relationship possible with both their parents and she would never deny her son that, no matter the personal cost to herself.

And it was costing her a lot.

'So you'll come?'

She strained every muscle in her face to form a

smile. She'd spent weekends with Nikos at his homes in Ibiza, Barcelona, Rome and London, while work commitments had forced her to turn down invitations for weekends at his homes in Mallorca and Athens, but the one home she'd longed for an invite to had never come. His real home. The island where he'd been born and raised. The island his family lived on. Mykonos.

'Sure. We'll come.'

His face widened into a grin, eyes glittering. 'Excellent. I will make the arrangements.'

# CHAPTER SIX

NIKOS FOLDED HIS arms across his chest and eyeballed his club manager. 'Did I, or did I not make it clear when I employed you that my clubs have a zero-tolerance policy on drugs?'

Toni's face was a classic mixture of fear and wounded pride. 'We do our best. We can't be held responsible for everyone who comes in.'

Nikos leaned across his desk. He'd deliberately not invited Toni to sit. 'And that's where we disagree. You have let the issue slip in my absence.'

'I didn't—'

'Do not interrupt me. Whatever our clients take before they enter our premises is nothing to do with us unless they are visibly wasted but the rules of the club are simple. Each guest is searched upon entry. All drugs are confiscated and destroyed. Those who refuse are themselves refused entry whether they're an office worker or a rock star. Those who don't like the rules are welcome to party in other establishments.' He held up the bag he'd swiped from a young lad on the dance floor. 'There must be a hundred pills in this. Let in on *your* watch. You're fired.'

'It was one mistake,' Toni protested.

'I've been in touch with the authorities. In my absence there has been a steady increase of drug-related incidents linked with this club. It's clear to me that you've been running a policy of turning a blind eye. Those days are over. The buck stops with you. Now get out.'

Toni's jaw clenched. For a moment Nikos wondered if he would have to physically remove him but then he turned on his heel and stormed out, slamming the door behind him.

Toni was the second club manager he'd fired in five days. Both for the same reason. Nikos hadn't spent eighteen months 'dead' to bring down a drug cartel and stop them poisoning his guests with their evil substances for his own staff to allow those same substances onto his premises.

Dear God, it had been men like Toni the cartel had targeted and put under threat, men like Toni that Nikos had given up eighteen months of his life to protect. When his Madrid club manager had gone missing days after his London club had been set fire to, he'd immediately quadrupled security at his clubs and employed bodyguards for high-profile employees like Toni. *Including* Toni. He'd conference-called them to spell out the danger they were in and all he was doing to mitigate it. Which had been everything. He'd been too sickened with fear for his employees' lives to do anything less than everything.

And then he'd found the photo of Marisa and the sickening fear had turned to icy terror. For as long as he resisted the cartel's demands, no one connected to him would be safe.

Shaking off the memories that still felt too fresh for comfort, Nikos rose, straightened the sleeves of his shirt from beneath his suit jacket and left his office.

When he'd opened his first club, the one in Ibiza, other club owners had called him mad for refusing to turn a blind eye to drugs. Club-goers wouldn't set foot in a club where they couldn't take the fuel that allowed them to party all night long!

He'd proved them wrong. Lure in the best DJs, provide top facilities and an exclusive, hedonistic atmosphere and the club-goers would flock to you.

That night, as usual, his Barcelona club was heaving with clubbers.

Nikos entered the VIP section and gestured for a drink as he joined the old friends waiting to celebrate his resurrection with him. This was something he'd done during all the club visits so far; get the business side sorted first and then party hard. After eighteen months of solitude, he had a lot of partying to make up for.

Champagne and raucous conversation flowed. Beautiful women displaying their wares fluttered their eyes at him and drank flirtatiously through straws. He could take his pick of them. Hadn't he been looking forward to taking his pick and to the familiarity of the chase that had been missing for eighteen months? Two years if you counted the six months he'd been with Marisa. Not just with her but faithful to her.

But, just as when he'd sat in the VIP sections of his other clubs that week, Nikos had to actively force himself to have a good time. Despite all his best efforts, nothing worked. Instead of feeling a part of things, he felt like an observer on the outside looking in. It all just seemed so damned superficial. It was at times like this he found himself missing the physical aspect of life in the Alaskan mountains. There had been a purpose to felling a tree, stripping it and chopping it into firewood. Cathartic too. A means to release the demons that had plagued him in those long, long lonely months.

After all that solitude he should be ravenous for female company but, yet again, he felt absolutely nothing. Not one woman captured his interest. Not as much as a flicker of attraction.

Here he was reclaiming his life and all he could see when the scantily clad beauties paraded before him was Marisa.

Two more nights and she would be in Mykonos with him. The thought alone tightened his sinews and thickened his blood more than a whole nightclub of scantily clad women could do.

Their relationship hadn't come to a natural end, he now realised. The flame of desire between them hadn't been allowed to burn itself out and, until the flame extinguished itself naturally, he was stuck. He couldn't move on.

To hell with the complications of another, much shorter affair. To hell with never going back. Nikos wanted his *life* back and that couldn't happen while Marisa remained unfinished business.

Marisa held Niki securely as she disembarked from Nikos's private plane, grateful her son hadn't suffered on the flight. He'd flown for the first time only a month ago and had hated every minute of it. This time she'd been prepared and he'd spent the flight content.

A large black car was parked a short distance from them and her already erratic heart ballooned painfully to see the long, lean figure standing against it.

Nikos's presence in her life these last seven days had been reduced to two snatched, fleeting visits to see their son. His near absence had brought no relief. It shattered her that far from his distance giving her space to properly get her head around their situation, she still woke every morning having to assure herself that he *was* alive. She had to stop her hands grabbing her phone to call him just to hear his voice.

Worse was the way her heart had thrummed for the entirety of those short visits. Worse still was the way it leapt whenever he fixed his gleaming eyes on her. The way her pulse thrummed when his gaze lingered too long on her... *Dios*, it was a sensation she hadn't felt in so long and it was terrifying how pleasurable a sensation it was. No matter how hard she tried to find it again, the control she'd mastered around him and that had cracked in the restaurant seemed far out of reach.

He strode towards them, shades on, a wide smile on his stubbly face, dressed in faded jeans, a grey V-neck T-shirt and a battered leather jacket. She'd forgotten how good Nikos looked in jeans and she frantically beat away memories of the washboard stomach and snake hips beneath them.

She forgot to hold her breath when he pressed a hand to her hip and leaned in to brush his cheek to hers. A flash of warmth against her skin and an enticing dose of spicy cologne hit her senses at the same moment he scooped Niki from her arms and set about planting huge kisses over his face.

She had just enough sense to be grateful he'd taken their son from her. From that moment of bodily contact, her limbs had weakened into mush.

'Comfortable trip?' he asked casually.

She semi-successfully curved her lips into a smile. 'Thanks for sending your plane for us.'

Holding Niki securely around his belly, he lifted him above his head. 'Only the best for my son and his mama.'

Their luggage had already been whisked into the boot of the car. A baby car seat had been installed in the back and Nikos strapped him in as if he'd done it a thousand times. The seat was so large it shrank the spacious interior.

The minute the door of the car enclosed them all inside she regretted not sitting up front beside the driver. Nikos's cologne filled the cabin, the bulk of his body, which was placed between her and their son, taking up almost as much space as the car seat. From the corner of her eye she saw him remove his jacket. For the first time since his return, she could see his arms and the contours of his body, and she pressed herself closer to the door and fought her greedy eyes' attempts to stare at him.

Was she imagining that, without a suit to hide most of his spectacular body, he was more muscular than she remembered?

She crossed her legs away from him and breathed through her mouth.

Soon they were driving through narrow streets in pretty towns with thick white walls and colourful roofs. She focused her attention on the nearing Aegean Sea, glimmering brightly under the setting sun, and tried to tune out the man who sat beside her.

'He's asleep.'

Nikos sounded so put out by this that she found herself smothering an unexpected giggle. 'He always falls asleep in cars.'

'There is still much for me to learn about him.'

'You know all the important things. Everything else is just window dressing.'

There was a long pause.

'Thank you.'

She turned her face to him before she could stop herself. 'For what?'

'For bringing him here.' His smile was wry but there was a softness in his eyes. 'I know it can't be easy for you to accept me into your lives when you spent all that time thinking I was dead. The way you've handled things has been incredible. When I think of everything you've been through, with the cartel and losing your father the way you did… I know how close you were to him.'

A lump formed in her throat and she had to swallow hard to speak past it. Losing her father on the heels of losing Nikos had ripped at the fabric of her sanity. 'It hasn't been easy. If not for Niki…'

'If not for Niki…?' he prompted when she stopped her words from running away from her.

The weight of his stare pressed on her chest.

'He pulled us together,' she said quietly. 'Getting through the rest of the pregnancy and preparing for his birth gave us focus. Mama…' She shook her head and looked back out of the window, trying her hardest to keep control of the words falling from her lips. 'Grief is like swimming through a black cloud and when it's someone you loved with all your heart and who you'd imagined yourself growing old with, it's a physical bruise that hurts with every breath you take. But having a child forces you to be strong, whether the child's an unborn baby or an adult. The primal urge to protect them is too powerful and so you pack away the pain and grief just to get through the days. You pack away *all* feelings. Bury them.'

And never let them out again.

Suddenly afraid her control had failed and she'd revealed too much about herself, she added as temperately as she could manage, 'That's how Mama got through it…how she *gets* through it. The only emotions she allowed herself were maternal ones. She was like a tiger roaring to keep her cubs safe.'

It had been like that for both of them. Two bereaved souls trying desperately to keep their heads above water enough to stop their children drowning with them.

Her skin prickled at the intensity of Nikos's probing stare that she could sense was trying to penetrate her skull to read her mind but the next time he spoke was as they approached a small village and he casually mentioned they'd reached his land.

Not until the car stopped in front of a sprawling three-storey, square-roofed villa did she realise the village was one huge interlinked complex. She counted ten properties surrounding the main villa in a horseshoe formation, all a pristine white.

She got out and felt a sigh of pleasure form in her throat. Surrounded by gentle rolling hills with the sea lapping to the rear, Nikos had made himself a home in paradise.

Hot tears stabbed the back of her eyes and her pleasure soured. How she'd longed to come here in the months when she'd been head over heels in love with him. She'd dropped enough hints but they must have been too subtle because he'd never picked up on them. Always he'd had a reasonable excuse not to invite her to accompany him on his visits home. She'd swallowed it every time and suppressed the nagging doubts that if he was as serious about her as she believed, he would want to show his main home off to her.

Deep down she'd known he didn't want her here. If she hadn't she would have gone further than drop hints. She would have asked him outright.

By not doing that she hadn't had to deal with his certain rejection. She could continue believing they were meant to be together.

She'd opened her home to him. Her family had opened their hearts to him. He'd failed to reciprocate and she'd ignored it. How had she been so wilfully blind?

Nikos carried his son from the back of the car. Marisa was staring at his home with her arms tightly folded. The last of the sun's rays poured on her, turning her hair into a curly golden halo. Her beauty was something that never failed to dazzle him and now that he was resolved on the path he intended to take with her, he welcomed the fizz her presence put in his veins.

'What do you think of my home?' he asked when he joined her.

She dropped her arms and blinked, but before she could answer, Niki decided the time was right to throw himself into his mother's arms. Like a slippery eel, he dived out of Niko's hold to her. If Nikos hadn't had such a good grip on him and if Marisa's reflexives weren't so honed, their son would have hurtled head-first to the ground. In the blink of an eye, the pair of them were holding their son sandwiched between, Marisa's breasts crushed against their interlinked arms.

For the briefest moment, time stood still.

Nikos found his gaze locked onto her wide eyes. Her face tilted, lips parted in frozen shock. And then he saw the colour creep over her cheeks and her throat move, and the compulsion to cover her parted lips and kiss her so thoroughly that she couldn't stand sent a rush of heat flooding through him.

Because, in that brief moment of triumph, Nikos's strong suspicions were confirmed.

His mouth curled into a slow smile.

Marisa's attraction to him was still there. He could practically taste it.

A warm beat echoed in Marisa's head. She didn't know if it was shock at her son's daredevil antics or being trapped in Nikos's stare that was causing it. At that moment, all she knew was that he was gazing at her as if he wanted to eat her whole.

She was brought back to her senses by her son, merrily jiggling between his parents' crushed bodies, oblivious that he'd been nanoseconds from a fractured skull, waving his arms around and smacking her in the face.

'Niki,' she chided, disentangling an arm from Nikos's hold to gently take her son's wrist. Niki grabbed her hair with his other hand. Before she could remove it, Nikos took the offending hand.

'Leave Mama's hair alone.' He pressed even closer to her to unpluck the little fingers clutching her hair.

Sensation brushed from the tips of her hair and danced into her skin. Her already thrashing heart went into overdrive and she held her breath, trying her hardest not to inhale his scent.

He smoothed her hair back into place and looked down at her. His eyes glimmered, a smile spreading over his face before he finally stepped away from her with a murmured, 'That was close.'

She breathed deeply and swallowed, jiggling Niki on her hip, trying her best to look serene, trying her best to appear oblivious to the current of heat that had just passed between them.

But she couldn't deny the expression in Nikos's eyes, not when she'd seen it so many times before, right before he would crush his lips to hers and make passionate love to her.

She tightened her hold on Niki and willed her heartbeats to stop crashing against her chest.

It was a look he must have given to hundreds of women in his time. If she hadn't been a naive virgin finally ready to fall in love, she would have known she was nothing special to him a long time ago and better protected herself.

Romance and love had never been on her radar. From her earliest days Marisa had wanted to join the family business and had taken seriously her father's decree that she must work hard and earn her place in it. Unlike her sister and most of her friends, she'd studied hard at school and had rarely bothered with boys. School holidays in her teenage years had been spent shadowing her father as he'd gone about his business.

She'd studied at Valencia University so she could continue learning everything about the business while she completed her business degree. She hadn't been entirely single-minded but she had been very focused, and when she'd graduated and taken her place at her father's side, she'd had the best of all worlds—a great career and a wonderful circle of friends. She hadn't wanted or needed more.

And then she'd met Nikos and fallen head over heels in love.

He'd turned to the smartly dressed man who'd appeared from the house. Nikos introduced him as Angelos, his butler, and then they were swept inside where a handful of staff waited for introductions in the large reception area.

Marisa tried to pay attention to their names but was too taken with the villa's interior. Even Niki stopped wriggling in her arms to gawp. Where her home in Valencia was traditionally Spanish with plenty of colour, this was almost exclusively white, from the thick, high walls to much of the furniture. Only the hard floor beneath her feet differed in being a pale, warm grey. And yet there was nothing cold about it.

Where her home had defined rooms with doors leading from one to the other, this had defined spaces reached through open arches, and she followed Nikos through one into a huge living space with four separate sofa areas. Through another arch in the far distance she could see the sea...

No longer waiting for Nikos to guide her, she shifted Niki in her arms and headed for the arch. Stepping through it, she found herself in a vast living space that extended seamlessly to an equally vast terrace. Open-mouthed, she slowly craned her neck from left to right, taking in the long infinity pool that lapped inside and then seemed to stretch out to the Aegean itself.

The hairs on the nape of her neck rose before Nikos's voice rumbled in her ear. 'What do you think?'

'It's stunning.'

He grinned and stepped onto the terrace, beckoning for her to follow. 'Let me show you the grounds.'

Marisa tried her best to pay attention to the tour itself rather than her tour guide, but her attention grew increasingly fractured. Not only did she have to concentrate on holding a bored baby in her arms but Nikos kept close enough to her that her senses threatened to go into overdrive. At one point he even rested a hand on her back when showing her the playground he'd had installed for their son and then, when he took Niki from her, his eyes held hers with the gleam in them that never failed to make her belly melt.

She could only manage appreciative murmurs at the spa and business centre situated in two of the smaller villas, the open-air cinema, the soft play room for Niki near the shallow end of another swimming pool so large a holiday resort would be proud to have it.

When they returned to the villa, a matronly figure stood with the butler waiting for them with a small suitcase at her side.

Nikos shook her hand, spoke to her in Greek then

made the introductions. 'Marisa, this is Seema. I've employed her as Niki's nanny for your stay here.'

Nikos watched Marisa's dark brown eyes widen before her gaze darted from him to Seema then back again.

'Pleased to meet you,' she murmured, extending a hand.

'Pleasure to meet you too,' Seema replied shaking the offered hand. Then she spoke to their son. 'You must be Niki.'

To his surprise, Niki shied away from her and buried his face in Nikos's shoulder. No amount of coaxing would get him to look at her.

'This isn't like him,' he said to Marisa. 'Usually he's so sociable.'

She shook her head tightly. 'He always needs time to get used to new people.'

'He took to me straight away,' he pointed out.

She shrugged. 'You're the only one. Maybe it's because on some weird baby level he recognised you as his father.' Then, as Nikos was puffing up with pride at her observation, she addressed the nanny. 'Don't worry, he'll be comfortable with you very soon but he's in a new country in a home that is strange to him. I'll take care of him tonight and then tomorrow we'll introduce the two of you again.'

Seema looked to Nikos for approval. His orders to her had been clear—she would be responsible for his son's routine that week, especially with regard to evenings and nights. As he could also feel Marisa's laser stare piercing through him, he nodded. 'Angelos will show you to your room and make you familiar with everything. If we need you this evening we'll page you.'

She bowed her head and disappeared with his butler.

There was a moment of silence before Marisa said, 'You've employed a nanny?' Her low tone did not disguise the underlying menace in it.

He met her flinty stare. 'Obviously.'

Her eyes narrowed and glinted. 'You had no right.'

He bristled. 'I had every right. I'm his father.'

'And I'm his mother and I'm only here *because* I'm his mother.'

'Seema has impeccable references. She was nanny to the King of Agon's children.'

'I wouldn't care if she came gold-plated! You had no right to go over my head like that, no right at all, and don't quote the "I'm his father" line at me again; you don't know Niki well enough yet to know what's in his best interests.'

'*Whose* best interests?' he disputed coolly. Nikos had been prepared for Marisa's annoyance about the nanny but her line of attack on the matter was out of order. 'His or yours?'

Angry colour stained her cheeks. 'How dare—'

'You hardly let him out of your sight. Even when we were organising the business partnership you brought him along to all the meetings. You do everything for him. When it comes to our son, you're a control freak.'

The dark circles under her eyes proved how much

she needed a break but a break would never happen if she had to get up at the crack of dawn each day to care for their son. He'd spent enough time with Mother Marisa to know she wouldn't trust him to care for Niki on his own. Not yet. She'd get up and hover between them.

That employing a nanny to care for their son left more time and opportunity for seduction was only secondary...

The baring of her teeth made him quite sure that she would have slapped him if he didn't have Niki in his arms.

'Caring for Niki is *my* job,' she snarled.

'You never relax or take time for yourself.'

'I'm a mother. It comes with the territory.'

His chest tightened as the image of his own mother floated in his mind and before he could stop himself he said, 'Not for all mothers.'

Not all mothers were tigers who roared to keep their cubs safe, like Marisa and her mother. Not all mothers had a primal urge to protect. Some mothers looked at their children and felt nothing.

Marisa's angry stare tempered, became contemplative. The piercing of the laser burn lessened as the composure he'd had so much fun cracking since her arrival visibly reset itself.

In a much calmer tone, she said, 'In future, please consult me before making any decision about our son's care.'

'Does that work for me too?' he challenged. 'Only

it seems that you're the one who gets to make all the decisions for him.'

'That's because I'm the one who raised him without his father for eleven months. I earned that right.' Then she looked at their son and her features softened. 'But I take your point. If you disagree with my judgements then we should discuss it.'

'Who gets the final say?'

'Logic does. Failing that, *me*.'

Nikos had to control every muscle in his mouth to stop it from opening and biting back some home truths to her. He was acutely aware that, though their son couldn't understand what they were saying, he would undoubtedly be picking up on the tense atmosphere between them. He would not allow Niki to witness any kind of war between his parents.

Swallowing back the rancid taste on his tongue, he indicated the winding staircase. 'I'll show you to your rooms.'

# CHAPTER SEVEN

Marisa held Niki close as she stepped over the threshold of the door Nikos opened for her in the wide corridor, using his solid little body as a shield to protect herself from the emotions thrashing and crashing inside her.

She'd known it would happen one day soon, that Nikos would assert his authority as a father, but she'd surprised herself at the strength of her feelings about it. Until that moment, every single decision about Niki had been made by her and her alone. Nikos had been dead! The times when she'd been uncertain about something she'd sought her mother's advice but the ultimate decision had always been hers. His sudden assertion of parental authority while she was fighting the effect his nearness was having on her had made her angrier about it than she should have been… And his reasons for it.

Why would he employ a nanny for her benefit? Why would he care if she took time for herself? She *knew* he didn't care a jot for her…

But he still wanted her. Hadn't she known that

since their meal together? And hadn't she sensed it before that?

His desire was there in every gleam of his eyes, a sensual promise that lived as a hum in her veins.

He didn't care for her but he still desired her as a woman, and, as she gazed around the room that would be hers for the week, she caught a glimpse of her reflection in a full-length mirror. For a moment she stared at the woman with the child in her arms.

A mother. A daughter. A sister.

A woman.

And then she caught Nikos's eye in the reflection. The icy steel she'd seen during their brief, heated argument had melted. What she saw in his light brown gaze now...

Her abdomen turned to liquid.

Marisa quickly looked away and forced her attention back to the room. It was as vast and white as the rest of the place but there were colourful feminine touches in the soft furnishings. The splashes of colour were the reds and oranges she adored, colours she hadn't seen in any other part of his home. Had these colourful touches been added for *her*...?

She couldn't stop her eyes darting back to Nikos. He stood by the glass door in the centre of the far wall, which had floor-to-ceiling windows, watching her.

'What do you think?' he asked.

She had to swallow hard to get her throat moving. 'It's perfect, thank you.'

The returning gleam had her tightening her hold

around their son, who, oblivious to the undercurrents happening around him, was merrily babbling away as he took in the newness of his surroundings.

Suddenly desperate to escape the intimate confines, she backed to the door. 'Where's Niki sleeping?'

He stepped away from the wall, a knowing half-smile playing on his lips. 'The room opposite. It's been turned into a nursery for him. I'll show you.'

If she didn't have Niki in her arms, she'd have run out of the room.

The nursery was a big hit with Niki, who immediately went crawling to the building blocks set out on the floor for him. The adjoining dressing room had been filled with brand new clothing and all the toys a baby on the cusp of his first birthday could wish for. As dinner would soon be ready, Marisa decided a change of clothes for him was needed. All the travelling had made their son grubby. It might have proved a great distraction from Nikos if he hadn't stood next to her at the baby changing table so he could make funny faces at their son while she put a new outfit on him.

He stood so close—deliberately, she was sure of it—that her lungs contracted. She could feel the heat of his skin vibrating against hers and a job that should have taken two minutes doubled because her brain forgot how to work her fingers and thumbs.

As she fumbled to get socks onto her son's plump feet, Nikos's phone vibrated and he stepped away from her.

She met her son's bright happy eyes and blew out all the air she'd been holding in one long puff, trying to make it into a joke for fear that if she didn't, she would burst into tears. They wouldn't be sad tears. They would be frustrated tears. Frustration at herself for still hungering and responding so desperately to the man who'd treated her so abominably.

'My grandfather's back,' Nikos announced. 'Is Niki ready?'

She pasted a smile to her lips, nodded and stepped aside to let Nikos pick him up.

Following them out of the room, she vowed to get a grip on herself. With this firmly in mind, she said, 'When you say he's back, does your grandfather live here?'

'He lives in the villa next to the spa. He could have had a wing in here but he likes privacy to entertain his lady friends.'

'I didn't realise,' she said evenly, descending the stairs in step with him. He'd never mentioned his grandfather living with him.

'What, that my grandfather still has an active sex life? It's something I try not to think about.'

A welcome kernel of laughter tickled her throat at his deadpan comment. 'No, that he lives with you. Is that a recent thing?'

'He moved in when I finished the renovations eight years ago.'

'What made you buy it? Was it the views?'

There was a tightness to his smile. 'I inherited it from my mother.'

She was instantly confused. 'I thought you grew up in Chora?' Chora was Mykonos's capital and she distinctly remembered him saying it was the part of the island he was from.

'This was my home until I was six.'

'That must have been quite a change for you.' Nikos's beachside villa was incredibly remote. 'Did you move for school?'

'No. My grandfather took custody of me,' Nikos replied shortly. 'He took care of me as a child and now I take care of him.'

Shock had her tightening her grip on the bannister. *Custody?*

But there was no time to ask what he meant by this for he increased his pace to greet the elderly gentleman waiting for them.

Nikos's grandfather, Stratos, was a man of, Marisa guessed, around eighty. He had a shock of white hair, a weather-beaten face, twinkling blue eyes and, from the way he bounded to them, the energy of a man half his age.

When Nikos made the introductions, she was taken aback to see the blue eyes turn to ice as they landed on her. His kiss to her cheek came with a definite coolness that immediately put her on edge. She was old enough to know that everyone couldn't like each other but this was the first time since her school days she'd detected such an instant and noticeable dislike of her.

What on earth had she done to cause it? Could it

be something as simple as Stratos being prejudiced against the Spanish or redheads?

If it was prejudice causing his frostiness to her, she was relieved to find his attitude didn't extend to her son.

Stratos couldn't speak Spanish or English. Marisa understood Greek far better than she spoke it—teaching herself Nikos's language so she could teach it to her son had been her greatest joy during her pregnancy—so that meant any ice-breaking conversation was out, but he didn't need verbal conversation to communicate with his great-grandson.

At first, Niki was as shy with him as he'd been with the nanny Nikos had hired. Stratos was undeterred, parking himself on the hard floor where he waited patiently for Niki's confidence around him to grow and was soon rewarded by his great-grandson using him as a human climbing frame.

Not once during this did he look at or attempt to communicate with Marisa.

Nikos did, though. Though she kept her stare on the two generations playing on the floor, she could feel his gaze burning into her. She wished the burn didn't feel like buzzing velvet in her veins. Wished her skin didn't shiver with awareness of his presence. She'd been wishing these things since he'd come back into her life.

Her mind kept going over his throwaway comment about his grandfather having custody of him. How had she spent six months of her life loving someone without knowing something so fundamental about them? The few things he'd revealed about his past had been delivered matter-of-factly before he'd turned the conversations around to her. It had been done in such a subtle way that at the time she'd preened under the weight of his thirst for knowledge about every aspect of her life. Now she realised it had been a deflection to stop her asking questions about him.

But these were thoughts that had to be put on the backburner when dinner was served and they all headed out to the table on the terrace to sit beneath the warm night sky.

Stratos took the seat next to the highchair and insisted on feeding Niki the specially prepared mush. The utter disgust on her son's face as the concoction hit his taste-buds was photo-worthy. He spat it out, globules of green goo landing on Stratos's white shirt.

For the first time since their introduction, the elderly man met her eye. He burst into loud, gravelly laughter that set her off too.

'Has that got courgette in it?' she asked when they'd all stopped laughing and Niki had been pacified with a bread roll and a banana and Stratos had gone back to ignoring her.

Nikos grinned. This was his first shared meal with his son in his own home. He would never have imagined a month ago that something so simple and ordinary could provoke such huge enjoyment.

He'd shared plenty of meals in Valencia with his son but they'd all been with Marisa and her family.

As outwardly welcoming and obliging as her mother and sister—on the occasions she'd joined them—had been to him, he'd known perfectly well that both of them would have cheerfully stabbed him with their forks if they'd thought they could get away with it. Strangely, he'd never had that vibe from Marisa, but then he remembered that in those first weeks she'd worn her indifference like armour.

He wondered if she was aware how greatly that armour had been stripped away. Or if she realised that every time she spoke to him, her fingers captured one of the ringlets splayed over her shoulders?

Seated diagonally from her, the pleasure of the evening was intensified by the enjoyment of her lovely face as his vista throughout the meal. Marisa was a beautiful woman but under the rising moonlight, her beauty turned into something other-worldly.

'I've no idea what the chef made him,' he answered after a drink of his wine. 'I should have warned him not to put courgette in his food.'

'You can add peppers and aubergine to the list,' she said without looking at him, fingers tugging on a ringlet. 'I made a batch of baby-friendly ratatouille a few days ago and you'd have thought I was trying to poison him.'

'I'm still amazed you can cook.'

'Only baby food,' she hastened to remind him, eyes darting to his before quickly looking away again.

Yet another example of her devotion to their son.

His own mother had never, to Nikos's recollection, cooked him a meal. She'd generally been too busy cooking her drugs to worry about feeding her son, and it rolled like poison in his guts to imagine his own son, belly cramping with hunger, teetering on a kitchen stool to reach a cupboard for food.

*Theos*, what was it about fatherhood that made the past feel more vivid and present than it had in decades?

Not just fatherhood. Marisa. The diametric opposite of his own mother but with the same power over her son in her hands.

He swallowed the poison away with more wine, determined not to ruin this evening by allowing thoughts about his mother and the past to intrude.

The main course over, staff cleared their dishes away. Marisa got to her feet. 'I need to put Niki to bed.'

'Stay for dessert?' he coaxed.

She shook her head while unclasping the high-chair straps keeping their son contained. 'It's way past his bedtime.'

Loving the way her silhouette played under the moonlight, Nikos looked her up and down. 'Seema can put him to bed tomorrow night and you can stay with the grown-ups.'

She didn't rise to the bait, lifting Niki from the highchair. 'I like to put him to bed myself.'

'You like to do everything yourself.'

'Only when it comes to this little one.' She leaned Niki towards Stratos so he could kiss his great-grandson goodnight then placed a polite kiss of her own to his wrinkled cheek.

Nikos watched her subtly brace herself before she carried their son to him. He took full advantage of her nearness, slipping an arm loosely around her back to keep her close. 'Goodnight, *moro mou*,' he said to his son as he smacked kisses over his face. When Marisa attempted to step away from him he trailed his fingers to her hips and slipped a finger into the pocket of her snug linen trousers. 'Don't *I* get a goodnight kiss, *agapi mou*?'

Her features tightened as her face made the tiniest of jerks before she found her composure and turned her flashing eyes on him. 'Of course.'

He heard the breath she took before she lowered her face, their son in her arms making her movements careful. As her plump lips made light contact with his cheek he turned his face and their lips brushed. The moment of contact was fleeting but enough for him to taste the heat from her mouth. Heady warmth unfurled in him and coiled through his bloodstream.

Face bathed with colour, blinking rapidly, holding their son like a shield, she stepped away from him. When her eyes met his again there was dazed accusation in them.

'Goodnight, *agapi mou*,' he murmured, holding the stare. 'Sleep well.'

She took another step back then inclined her head and turned. Moments later, she disappeared inside.

It took a few more moments for Nikos to pull himself together.

Shifting in his seat, Nikos topped up his and his grandfather's wine glasses.

'Your son is going to be a real character,' his grandfather said with a chuckle.

Nikos smiled in response and took a large drink of his wine. His blood still pumped unexpectedly hard from the effects of the fleeting kiss.

'I never thought I would live to meet a great-grandchild, least of all from you.'

Nikos was an only child but had a dozen cousins he'd run amok around Chora with. He kept in touch with a few of them and the rest he saw at the usual family events of christenings, weddings and funerals. 'It was as big a surprise to me as to you.'

His grandfather's gaze became serious. 'You need to marry her.'

Nikos's good mood ended with those five words. 'That isn't necessary.'

'You won't think that if she stops you seeing him.'

'Marisa wouldn't do that,' he refuted automatically.

'You don't know that for sure. I raised you but she didn't tell me about him, and don't tell me she didn't know how to, she had the means and money to contact me if she'd wanted, and she has the means and money to fight you if she decides to stop you seeing him.'

'She loves him too much to do anything but what's best for him.' But his grandfather's cynical words had set off a pounding in his head. Hadn't similar thoughts already occurred to him?

'Her opinion on what's best might mean keeping him from you. What *is* best for him—and you—is having parents who are married.'

'My parents were married. That was hardly best for me.'

His grandfather winced. 'That wasn't marriage's fault. That was the drugs' fault.'

'They hated each other with or without the drugs.' And neither had cared a jot for him, he thought with a stab.

'They loved each other once. It was the drugs that ruined them.'

Nikos bit back his temper. He wasn't prepared to fall into another argument about it. His grandfather had a more sympathetic view of the past. Nikos supposed that was Stratos's love for his son still wanting to see the best in him despite all the evidence to the contrary.

'I only remember them as being at war with each other. I'm not going to put Niki through that. We'll formalise a custody arrangement when he's old enough to be parted from her for periods of time.'

'And when will that be?' his grandfather challenged. 'Do you see the way she is with him? She watches him like a hawk. It will be years before she allows you to have him without her.'

The ring of truth in his grandfather's words reminded him of how the colour had drained from her face when he'd asked if Niki could come to Mykonos. The colour had only returned when he'd clarified he meant for her to come too. He remembered, too, her earlier reaction to him employing a nanny. By her own admission, Marisa liked to do everything for their son. She did not like her judgement on his welfare to be challenged.

But marriage?

'You will have to hope she's amenable to a formal arrangement,' his grandfather added into the silence.

'She will be.' But Nikos's words sounded unconvincing to himself.

'I know you hate the idea of marriage but, remember, it doesn't have to last for ever.'

He flickered his eyes to his grandfather. His marriage to Nikos's grandmother, had been tragically cut short by her death from ovarian cancer four decades ago. Stratos had never said it in words but from the little he *had* said, Nikos had intuited the marriage had not been a happy one. His grandfather had enjoyed many lady friends since his wife's death but had never remarried or lived with another woman.

By the time his grandfather retired to bed, the doubts Stratos's words had sown had solidified his own fears into weights in his guts.

Too uptight to sleep, Marisa, baby monitor in hand, opened the glass door in her room and stepped out onto the balcony.

Putting the monitor on the wrought-iron table, she stepped to the balustrade and breathed deeply as she gazed out at the Aegean lapping on Nikos's private beach in the near distance. If she inhaled hard enough the faint salty tang might clear her mouth of the taste of Nikos that no amount of minty toothpaste could eradicate.

A throb of heat pulsed in her abdomen. Their lips had connected for barely a second but that second had been long enough for their breath to meld together and for any hope of control to be shattered.

She wriggled her shoulders to fight the shiver lacing her spine as she replayed the sensual tone of his voice when he'd bidden her goodnight, and forced her attention on her surroundings rather than the melting mess she was in danger of turning into. Look at the stars! See how they reflected off the black sea. See how they shone so brightly. The Valencian suburb the Lopez estate was located in was renowned for its wealth and beauty but it had nothing on Nikos's home. This had everything, beauty *and* peace.

What secrets were contained within its boundaries?

Many secrets. She was certain of it.

She'd intuited his childhood had been very different from the happy idyll of her own, but never had she guessed it had been bad enough that his grandfather had taken custody of him. He'd never even hinted at it. All she'd really learned about his childhood was that he'd lived and gone to school in Chora until he was fourteen, when he was sent *by his family*, as he'd put it to her, to boarding school in England, and the names of his childhood friends, many of whom he was still in contact with.

She squeezed her eyes shut in an attempt to drive Nikos's image away. She'd come out here to clear her mind, not think about him even more.

But not thinking about him was impossible when she could feel his presence in the buzz of her veins and when so many old familiar feelings were blossoming and singing and anticipation quivered low in her pelvis.

When she opened her eyes, she noticed for the first time that the long, wide balcony stretched further than the limits of her room. Tightening the sash of her satin robe, she followed her curiosity to the end of it and discovered the balcony was shared with the room next to hers. The curtains running the length of the glass wall were drawn but that didn't stop her taking a step back and then quickly padding back to her own half.

Tingles danced over her skin as instinct told her the adjoining room was Nikos's.

# CHAPTER EIGHT

IT WAS LATE when Nikos carefully opened the nursery door and tiptoed to the cot. Staring down at the innocent sleeping form, he lightly stroked his son's soft cheek as his mind ran through the myriad ways Marisa could keep them parted if she so chose. It was all he'd thought about since his grandfather had vocalised the unease that had been steadily building inside him about Marisa's power.

She did have the money and the means to make life as difficult as she wanted it to be for him to see his son. She loved their son in a way his mother had never loved him, and if his own mother could turn her back on him, what was there to stop Marisa from doing the same? Her wealth didn't compare to his but when coupled with her protectiveness of their son and the imperious majesty she could turn on like a tap, it would make her a formidable opponent if she chose to fight him.

Nikos had never backed down from a fight in his life but those fights had never had a flesh and blood child at its centre. His own childhood had been wrecked by neglectful, warring parents and, though this situation was very different, he would do everything in his power to stop his son going through anything remotely the same.

However much the concept of marriage turned his stomach, it would give him greater authority and legal protection, and make the custody issue smoother when they eventually divorced. More civilised.

He bent over and kissed his son's forehead. 'Sleep well,' he whispered.

Niki had been a part of his life for such a short time but already he knew that, for his child, he would do anything. Even marry his mother. And in the process stop her ever having the opportunity to take his son from him.

Now all he had to do was convince Marisa, and as he closed the nursery door behind him, his lips curved into a smile and his skin prickled with arousal as he imagined the most effective way of getting her agreement.

Marisa sat back on the plush heart-shaped seat in the corner of her balcony and took a deep breath to calm herself. Her heart had leapt into her mouth when the baby monitor's green light had flashed to indicate movement in the nursery. She'd been on the verge of charging into the room when Nikos's whispered voice had sounded through the monitor.

The cartel was defeated but the paranoia that had dogged her the last year lived on.

The semblance of peace she'd found on the balcony was further disturbed moments later when the door at the far end slid open and a shadow fell over the moonlit marble flooring.

Heart immediately striding into a canter, she hugged the satin robe she'd slipped over her short silk pyjamas tighter around herself and strove for nonchalance at Nikos's approach. The canter became a ragged thrum when she spotted the bottle of white wine and two glasses in his hands.

'I thought you were tired.' A smile played on his handsome face. A smile that made her belly turn to goo.

'I couldn't sleep.'

'This should help you.' He pulled up a chair by the table, positioned it close to her, opened the bottle and poured them both a glass. Gaze holding hers, he held one out to her. 'Here.'

She shouldn't. Definitely not. What she should do is wish him goodnight—again—and go back to her room and lock the door behind her.

They hadn't been alone together, not properly, not just the two of them, since the night of his return.

She absolutely should not allow herself to be alone with him under the moonlight.

She took the glass from him with murmured thanks and put it to her lips. It was crisp and delicious. Much like the man her eyes were locked on.

He gave another stomach melting smile and relaxed into his chair. He was sitting so close to her his knees were inches from her feet. 'What's on your mind?'

'Nothing important.' Seeing his eyebrow rise lazily at her obvious lie, she added, 'We share this balcony?'

'Yes. My room's next to yours.'

'Oh.'

'But you had already guessed that,' he said knowingly. 'You were waiting for me.'

The rush of heat to her cheeks was so excruciating she couldn't find the words to deny it.

Because his words were the truth.

She'd hurried away from his end of the balcony back to hers and sat on this very seat with a cocktail of emotions racing through her blood. The strongest had been anticipation. She just hadn't realised it until Nikos had vocalised it.

'Don't be embarrassed, *agapi mou*.' He put his glass on the table and leaned forward to take her bare foot in his hand and gently pull it onto his lap. 'I know it will be impossible for me to sleep knowing only a wall separates me from you.'

'I…' She tried to breathe. Tried to find the will to pull her foot away and drag her stare from his face.

Ever since Nikos had returned she'd done everything in her power to avoid his gaze. And this was why. Once caught in the depths of his light brown eyes there was no escape.

His fingers made feather-light circular motions over her toes.

Why wasn't she resisting?

'There's no shame in wanting someone,' he whispered. His circling movements reached her ankle. Flaming shivers licked her skin. 'Or shame in admitting defeat.'

She tried to snatch air in.

'We have both tried to fight the inevitable,' he continued with that same sensual huskiness in his voice. A finger slowly traced up the inside swell of her calf. 'It is like the tide fighting the moon.'

She wanted to deny it. Loudly. Scream that he was wrong.

But that would be her wounded pride screaming. Nikos had broken her heart then stamped on the shattered pieces for good measure. There was nothing left of her heart for him to damage.

Nikos saw the emotions play out over Marisa's face. He noticed every pulse in her eyes, every ragged movement of her chest. He saw the flush of colour on her cheeks and the way her breasts strained towards him and the outline of her nipples pressed against the fabric of her nightwear. And he saw the fight she was waging against herself.

His fingers crept to the sensitive flesh of her inner thigh. 'Do you still have feelings for me?'

Her throat moved but still she didn't speak.

He inched his seat a little closer, nudging her thighs apart with his knees as he swirled his fingers even higher. 'I still have feelings for you.' His fingers reached the hem of her silk pyjama shorts. 'I try to forget you but there has been no one since you.'

Her breaths were coming in short, ragged bursts.

When he slowly slipped a finger under the fabric of her shorts, her body trembled. He could feel the heat coming from the heart of her femininity and inched his thumb closer to the core.

She jolted, eyes widening.

'I've imagined us together so many times,' he whispered. He could see her trying to bring herself back into focus, and ran his thumb up the lips of her pleasure until he reached her swollen nub. Her back arched, breaths now coming in pants.

'I remember your scent.'

Keeping the pressure on her nub, he slid a finger inside her. Her head fell back. A soft moan escaped her lips.

'I remember your taste. I remember how good we were together.'

With a trembling hand she pulled the sash of her robe apart and then unbuttoned her pyjama top, exposing the breasts he'd once carelessly thought had been designed especially for him.

Then, breasts swaying with the motion, using her elbows as support, she lifted herself upright until she had a hand clutching the collar of his shirt and her molten brown eyes met his.

'Nikos...?' His name sounded like it had been dragged out from deep inside her.

Nikos was so turned on that now he was the one struggling to speak. 'Yes, *agapi mou*?'

She pressed her pelvis tighter against his hand and covered his free hand, lifting it and placing it on her breast. 'Stop talking and take me to bed.'

And then, still holding tightly to his shirt, her head fell back and she shuddered violently.

The tattoo of Marisa's heart drummed loudly in her ears as she fought for breath.

Her hand clutched Nikos's shirt like a vice. The strength of the orgasm that had just erupted within her should have drained the arousal from her but the ache in her core still throbbed.

Leaning closer to her, he moved his hand out from under her shorts and slowly wound it around her back.

She met the hooded stare with a frankness she had denied them both these past weeks. His lips were tightly set, nostrils flaring as he breathed in and out. His body had gone rigid.

She inched her face closer to his until she felt the heat of his skin against her own and the musky scent of his skin and the faint scent of his cologne soaked into her senses. She rubbed her nose against his cheekbone and breathed him in some more, releasing his shirt to bury her fingers into the soft dark hair and dig the tips into the back of his skull.

The fight was over. She had lost.

But she had won too. The incredible feelings ravaging her were proof of that.

For the first time since Nikos's death, she felt like Marisa again. A woman with desires and needs, not just a mother, a daughter, a sister.

The sensual side of her nature—a side only Nikos had seen—had been locked in hibernation since the day of his death and now he'd awoken it, unleashing the burn that had once seen her beg for his touch.

He couldn't hurt her again. She knew that now. The damage he'd caused was irreparable.

But he could give her pleasure. Pleasure like nothing else on this earth.

Nikos stared into the molten eyes still pulsing with the effects of her climax. Her body still trembled, her sweet breaths still ragged.

Arousal bit him so fiercely that the scrape of Marisa's nails against his skull was as effective as if she'd taken his excitement in her hand. It was a struggle to draw in the air he needed to temper it, a task made harder when every inhalation drew her scent into his lungs.

He needed to get hold of himself before he…

He sucked in a sharp breath as she pressed her cheek to his and dragged the hand not kneading his skull down to his hand and placed it back against her breast. The shallowness of her breaths whispering against his skin was as erotic as the feel of the plump weightiness in the palm of his hand.

*Theos…*

He gritted his teeth and closed his eyes against the deep throbbing in his loins.

Nineteen months of celibacy and the effect was to make him feel like an overly excited teenager about to bed a woman for the first time.

He hadn't felt such desire even then. The closest he'd come to feeling like that was the first time with Marisa. It had been the headiest, most erotic moment of his life. Her virginity and the length of time she'd forced him to wait for consummation had heightened the effects. That's what he'd thought. But it had only got better. And better. And better.

Nineteen months of celibacy but his body remembered. Every cell in his body pulsated in anticipation.

Eyes wide open and burning into his, her lips dragged slowly to his mouth and hovered, lips parted but only a whisper of connection between them. The sweet taste of her breath danced onto his tongue. Her fingers dug deeper into his skull.

The last thread holding him to the earth snapped and with a groan he had no control over, Nikos captured her beautiful lips in a kiss of pure, hedonistic savagery.

Tongues entwined, teeth grazed, fingers bit into flesh. There was little comprehension that she'd shifted her body until she was straddling his lap and their bodies were crushed together.

Clasping her bottom, he rose to his feet, lifting her with him. Her legs wound around his waist as he carried her through the open door to the turned-down bed.

In seconds he was lying on top of her, kissing and nipping, their hands working together in a frenzy to strip away the barrier of clothing. Shrugging his shirt off, he covered a breast with his mouth and greedily sucked and licked, hands wrenching at the silk shorts she'd dragged down to her hips, then worshipped her other breast as he worked the shorts to her knees. She kicked them off while her hands tugged at his unbuttoned trousers, sitting up to get a better grip before she yanked them down with his underwear until they were kneeling before each other, naked and panting with lust. For no more than a second they stared into each other's eyes. Nikos's arousal reached boiling point to see the unashamed desire in hers and the colour slashing her face.

He pounced. She pounced.

Their mouths locked together as he fell back on top of her.

Marisa's thighs parted with no thought from her brain. There were no thoughts. Only sensation. Such glorious, heavenly, mind-blowing sensations. The weight of Nikos on her, the feel of his skin against hers, his taste and scent on her tongue and infused in all her other senses…

The heat burning between her legs was almost too much to bear and when she felt the heavy weight of his erection right where she needed it to be, she moaned, '*Please*, Nikos. Please. Now.'

He drove inside her in one long, hard thrust.

The relief was so great that she cried out.

Arms wrapped tightly around his neck, legs hooked around his waist, mouth buried in his shoulder, Marisa closed her eyes and fell into the saturating pleasure.

Deeply he thrust into her, in and out, a fusion of heat and flesh driving each other on until she felt the thickening between her legs and clung even tighter as the pulsating ripples broke free and carried her to a peak that left her limp and boneless.

\* \* \*

A breeze came through the opened door. Nikos closed his eyes and welcomed its cooling touch. Marisa lay on her back beside him, the sheets pulled up to her shoulders. When he'd rolled off her she'd wriggled away from him. She'd made no effort to touch him since.

They hadn't exchanged a word since their explosion of lust. He didn't know about her but the thumps of his heart had been impossible to speak through. It was yet to settle back into a normal beat.

It had never beat normally around her...

He took a deep breath. That kind of thought was what had made him glad to end their relationship. Too many strange thoughts in the minutes and hours after making love.

In the aftermath of lovemaking back then, Marisa would always cuddle up to him. She would put her ear to his chest and, though it had gone unspoken, he'd known she'd been listening to his heartbeat. It had been the strangest feeling, unsettling and yet somehow comforting, the way she'd taken such pleasure from the beating of a heart. His heart. She would stroke his skin too. Nuzzle her nose against his chest. Stretch against him and tilt her head to smile at him. Whisper that she loved him. He'd never believed those words but to hear them had always filled his chest with so much emotion it had hurt his heart to breathe through it.

Now she might as well be a corpse for all the life he detected from her.

But she was awake. Marisa was too deep a sleeper to fake it. When sleep came for her, she rolled onto her side and curled into a ball. He'd always hated the loss of her warmth when she did that. Often he would wake and find he'd curled into her as if his sleeping body had subconsciously sought her out. He'd never done that with anyone else either.

'What are you thinking?' he asked.

There was a long period of silence before she answered. 'Why?'

'It's not like you to lie quietly after sex.'

'It's been a long time since we shared a bed, Nikos.' She sighed and turned her face to his. 'Shouldn't you go back to your own room?'

'Do you want me to?'

She looked back to the ceiling. 'I think it's best.'

'Why?'

'Sometimes Niki wakes early. I bring him back to bed with me.'

'Can't you do that with me here?'

'It would only confuse him.'

'Why?'

'It just would. I don't want him to think you and I are like other mamas and papas.'

'Isn't he too young to think like that?'

'I don't know what he thinks. He might have lots of fully formed thoughts in his head.'

'He might,' Nikos conceded. 'And one of those thoughts might be a wish for his mama and papa to live together.'

'Don't speak like that.' She rolled to the edge of the bed and slipped her robe on.

'Why not?' he challenged. 'Is that not a normal wish for a child?'

She tightened the sash and got to her feet. 'Nobody's normal is the same as anyone else's.' She stepped out onto the balcony. A moment later, the outside light was turned off and she came back in, closing the door behind her.

Using the dim light of the moon and stars to illuminate the way, she carried the baby monitor to her bedside table and sat on the bed with her back to him. 'I mean it, Nikos. I don't want to confuse him.'

'Neither do I.'

'Good.'

'I only want to do what's best for him, as I know you do.'

Her head dipped forward.

'Which is why I think we should consider marrying.'

The stiffening of her back, the slow turn of her body to face him, the wide eyes and open mouth were almost comical but the situation was too serious for him to find amusement in it. Now that the idea of marriage had rooted in his head, he knew he had an uphill battle to get Marisa's agreement but was confident he would succeed. All he had to do was pull the right strings.

As difficult as the task would be, there was already relief that the decision had been made. Nikos's feelings for his son grew by the day. He wanted to be a real father to him, with autonomy, not someone for Niki to visit a few times a year. He wanted the security of knowing his son could never be taken from him.

He could manage a year of marriage and then separate from Marisa knowing he had the right of being a father in the law's eyes on his side. Sure, she'd named him as the father on Niki's birth certificate but marriage gave him much greater protection. She wouldn't be able to deny his demand for equal access.

A year of marriage also meant a year of having Marisa in his bed and that brought relief of a different hue. Such a short time since they'd made love but already fresh awareness was coiling through him.

It had been like this before. His desire for her had intoxicated him. Almost driven him to madness.

A year of marriage would be long enough to spend his passion for her and allow them to reach the natural end his fake death had denied them.

Now all he needed to do was persuade Marisa to say yes.

# CHAPTER NINE

Marisa shook her head as if expelling water from her ears. She'd been holding onto herself by the skin of her teeth, desperately fighting the craving to lie in Nikos's arms and recapture the closeness she'd always adored after making love when he'd dropped his bombshell on her. He thought they should marry?

How was she supposed to process something like that? It would have been less of a shock if he'd told her he wanted fly to Jupiter and colonise it.

She stared at his dimly lit face, looking for a sign that he was joking. He lay stretched out on the bed, arms folded above his head, his gorgeous face expressionless, but she sensed him soaking in her shock, waiting for her to get herself together. It was an expression that made her hackles rise.

Shifting her entire body round to face him, she folded her arms tightly around her chest, afraid he would see the ferocious thudding of her heart. 'You think we should marry?'

'Yes.'

She shook her head again. 'What on earth for?'

'For Niki. For all of us.' He rolled onto his side and propped himself up on his elbow. 'Being away from you this week made me realise how much I need you both in my life. I want us to be a family, *agapi mou.*'

How she wished the strings of her heart didn't tug so hard at this. 'You've changed your tune.'

'I didn't know how much being a father would change my perspective on life. You had an idyllic childhood with a mother and father who were together and I want that for our son. Don't you want that for him too?'

She'd wanted that once, she thought with a deep wrench. She'd ached for it. Her early pregnancy had been spent clinging to the futile hope that Nikos was still alive, cast away on a desert island sending smoke signals and creating a giant SOS on a beach. He would be found. She would tell him of the pregnancy and he would drop to one knee, declare his love for her and they would live happily ever after.

But that hope had always been in vain, and she'd known it. He'd fallen overboard in the Mediterranean. His crew had discovered him missing the morning after a night anchored at sea in bad weather. The last person to see him alive reported he'd been standing on deck, watching the surrounding storm. The hunt for him had been one of the largest undertakings the region had ever seen. All the small uninhabited islands in the Balearics, the area in which he'd disappeared, were thoroughly searched numerous times. No body had been found.

The sea had swallowed Nikos up. Eventually, her heart had accepted this, as well as the knowledge that her son would never know his father. When her own father was subsequently murdered, she'd had to deal with the unimaginable pain of his death and the aching realisation her son would have no father figure in his life. Once, she'd hoped Raul might be the father figure Niki would come to need. Blind desperation for help with the business, and safety and protection for her son had seen her propose to him.

And now Nikos was offering her the one thing she'd always longed for from him and all she could think was that he hadn't cared to tell her he was alive and well until he'd learned about their son.

'Since when do you need me in your life?' she asked.

'Since I came back into it.' His gaze didn't falter. 'I thought we'd both moved on but what we've shared tonight is proof that what we had is still alive.'

Her pelvis clenched and blood thickened to remember exactly what they'd just shared and she pressed her thighs tightly together, doing everything she could not to allow all the internal sensations show on her face. 'Is that what tonight was about?' she asked as evenly as she could. 'A seduction to remind me how good we are together? To soften me up with sex so I'm more open to the idea of marriage?'

'Partly.'

She closed her eyes at the sting of his admission and turned away from him.

'But you can't deny the chemistry between us has been getting stronger,' he added into the silence. 'What we just shared was going to happen and it will happen again whether you agree to marry me or not.'

'Your ego is as big as ever,' she said shakily.

The mattress dipped. Tingles raced up her spine, breath catching as she felt him close the gap between them. When he placed his hands on her shoulders and pressed a kiss on the arch of her neck she had to clench her teeth to stop a moan escaping.

'Not my ego,' he murmured into her hair, pressing his chest into her back. 'The truth. And I know you feel it too.'

Nikos cupped a weighty breast and rubbed his thumb over a nipple that hardened at his touch.

'See?' he whispered. 'Already you want me again. There is not a minute when I'm with you when I don't fantasise about us being together like this.'

She caught hold of the hand manipulating flesh that had always been so sensitive to his touch. Her fingers dug into his skin and stilled as if in hesitation before lacing through his.

'This is just sex,' she said with a sigh.

'Good sex. Great sex. Just as we had before. Remember how good we were together? We can have that again.'

She yanked his hand off her breast and shuffled away from him. 'If we were so good together, why didn't you come back to *me*?'

He chose his words carefully, regretting his honesty in those hours after his return. If he'd known then what he knew now—if he'd *felt* then what he felt now—he would have handled things differently.

'You'd moved on. You were engaged to another man. I thought I'd moved on too but no one compares to you.' He closed the gap she'd created and put his hands on her hips. 'There has been no one but you since the day we met, and I know we can make it work. We can be a real family and give Niki the love and stability I never had.'

She was silent for a long time but he took comfort that she didn't pull away from him again.

'Tell me about it,' she said.

'What?'

Now she did pull away, stretching across the bed to put the bedside light on. Then she turned round to face him. 'Tell me about your childhood.'

'It's history,' he dismissed.

'*Your* history. If you want to marry me so Niki has the love and stability you never had, then I want you to tell me why. Explain it to me. Make me understand. Otherwise my answer is no.'

Nikos could see from the set of her jaw and her unwavering stare that Marisa wasn't bluffing. He cursed himself for unwittingly opening the goal for her to shoot into.

He'd never brought Marisa to Mykonos when they'd been dating because he'd needed to keep a separation between them. He'd never discussed his childhood, had always made it clear from the outset in any relationship that it was an off-limits subject. But Marisa was not like his other lovers. On the surface, she'd been of the same breed as the others. Glossy. Immaculate. But surfaces were deceptive and hers was more deceptive and far deeper than most.

The first obvious difference between her and his other lovers had been her refusal to go home with him that first evening. It hadn't been the refusal that had marked her as different but that she had meant it. Marisa hadn't been playing a game of hunt and chase. She'd had self-respect and he'd quickly come to respect her hugely for it. She'd got closer to him than anyone ever had, and it had been a battle to fight through the intoxication of their lovemaking to resist letting her get any closer.

He'd resisted bringing her to the home of his early childhood because he'd sensed she had the capacity to dig beneath the villa's glossy, immaculate exterior and bring the ugly truth into the light.

To bring Marisa here would have meant answering questions about a part of his life he preferred to forget.

His instincts back then had been right.

But his past had been pushing for air, swirling into his thoughts during his time in exile, the memories strengthening and blindsiding him ever since his son had come into his life.

Stomach churning, he leaned back to rest against the headboard. 'What do you want to know?'

'Everything. But we can start with your parents and why your grandfather took custody of you.'

He wanted to rip his gaze from her stare. Instead,

he straightened his spine and met it head on. 'My parents were drug addicts.'

There was a flickering in her eyes.

'You sure you want to hear this? It isn't pretty.'

'I'm sure.'

He shrugged. So be it. Maybe giving the memories the oxygen they wanted and Marisa wanted would be enough to silence them for ever.

'Don't misunderstand me—I don't want you to imagine a scene of squalor like the junkies that are portrayed in films. I mean, they *were* junkies, but they were high functioning. They were both clever, high maintenance individuals who needed a steady fix of narcotics to help them function.'

'You keep saying *were*? Are they both dead?'

'My father's alive but I haven't seen him in a long time. Fifteen years, maybe. My mother died ten years ago. She came from a wealthy family…' he waved his hand around to indicate the villa he'd inherited from her '…and was what in today's terms would be a socialite. My father was a musician. I'm told he was once an excellent one. They were both mild drug users when they got together but their influence on each other was destructive. They supposedly loved each other once but all I remember is them hating each other. They had many all-night parties here and would just erupt in front of everyone.' He laughed grimly. 'Everyone acted as if it was normal, two grown people throwing ornaments and threatening each other with knives…'

'What?' She interrupted, her set face suddenly cracking with horror. 'You *saw* this?'

'I witnessed a lot of violence and drug taking. I was put in my grandfather's custody when my mother smashed a glass over my father's head. He wasn't seriously injured but there was enough blood that one of their friends called for a doctor.'

He blinked away the memories of the blood pouring over his father's shocked face that moments before had been twisted in a goading snarl. Nikos had been playing with his stuffed elephant, making it ride his toy truck, and he remembered the sickening thuds of his heart as he'd pretended not to see or hear, just kept the elephant and truck circling and circling.

'The doctor saw me playing on the floor surrounded by vast quantities of drugs and felt dutybound to call the authorities. They took me away and gave me to my grandfather.'

'And you were *six*?' she asked faintly. Her face had turned ashen.

'Yes. It was agreed my parents' lifestyle wasn't conducive to raising a child and my grandfather agreed. I didn't know it then but he'd been fighting for custody of me for years. He'd never approved of what he thought of as their champagne lifestyle but his suspicions of drug use had been just that— suspicions. He had no hard evidence and my mother had the wealth and contacts to ban him from their home and put a stop to his interfering. Those were the days I presume she had some form of maternal feelings for me.' Those maternal feelings hadn't lasted long enough for Nikos to remember any sign of them.

'So overnight you were taken from your parents and given to your grandfather?' She shook her head. 'I can't even begin to understand how that must have felt.'

'You know what you just said about everyone's normal being different? Drug addicted parents who hated the sight of each other was my normal. It took a long time for me to understand and accept I would never live with them again.'

Months and months of nightmares.

His parents had been his world and he'd loved them. His life had centred round pleasing them. A smile from his mother or an absent pat on the head from his father had been enough to fill his childish heart with joy that would last for days.

His mute terror at the violence he'd witnessed between them and the ache in his heart when another night would roll around without a goodnight kiss had been nothing to his terror at being taken from them.

Marisa brought her knees up to her chin and tried to take it all in as dispassionately as Nikos had narrated it. It was impossible. All she could see in her mind's eye was a little dark-haired boy playing on the floor surrounded by stoned adults, drugs and blood. She saw faceless authority figures swooping in and leading him out of the only home he'd known by his hand, the little boy not knowing his world was on the cusp of changing for ever. Or that *he* was on the cusp of changing for ever.

'And when you did accept it…how did you find living with your grandfather?'

He pulled a face. 'Difficult. We both did. I'd had no discipline at all and was used to fending for myself. We clashed very badly, especially as I got older. He sent me to boarding school in England when I was fourteen. English boarding schools have a reputation for strictness. My mother paid for it.' His face twisted bitterly. 'She could have used her wealth to fight to keep me, paid others to care for me, all kinds of things she could have done to keep me under her roof, but she chose not to—turns out she found it preferable to live without the bother of a child. But she was more than happy to pay for me to move countries.'

Nausea churned in her belly. Nikos's observation that Marisa's childhood had been idyllic was true and something she'd always been aware of and thankful for. Compared to what Nikos had been through it had been served to her on a bed of rose petals carried by winged cherubs. Not for a single second had she wondered whether her parents loved her. Their love had been so deeply imbedded in her that there had never been a need to question it.

Struggling to speak, she whispered, 'What about your father?'

'Within months of me being taken from them, they split up and he left for the mainland. He's still there now, in Athens, I think, playing his guitar in restaurants. He snorted and smoked most of the money he got off my mother in the divorce.' A pulse throbbed on his jawline. 'You know, I grew to hate them. I mean, *really* hate them. Especially my mother. She had the money to fight for me. I had a small inheritance of my own from her parents. It was put under my grandfather's control.

'He gave me a sum of it when I turned sixteen. I lived independently off that money and turned it into a fortune while having the time of my life, and didn't return to Mykonos until I was twenty-three. I hadn't seen her in six, seven years and the change I saw in her was enormous. She'd had so much work done to her face that it looked plastic but it didn't hide the damage from her addictions and lifestyle. I still hated her but seeing her like that...' His lips tightened. 'I began to feel a responsibility to her.'

He laughed morosely. 'It is strange how we change, isn't it? I never thought I would feel that. A responsibility for that woman. But I did.'

'Maybe it was seeing her with adult eyes,' she suggested softly. 'You could see her vulnerabilities.'

'Maybe.' He shrugged. 'I got into the habit of calling her every few days. One day she didn't answer. I tried a number of times. I was in London and called the Mykonos authorities. They found her dead on her bedroom floor.'

Cold horror sliced through her heart.

'She'd overdosed.'

Marisa rubbed her mouth against her knee and closed her eyes to stop the threatening tears from falling. He didn't want her sympathy.

In the end, all she could think to say was the honest, simple truth. 'I'm sorry.'

Nikos swung his legs off the bed and opened the door to step onto the balcony.

He needed air.

Fingers tight around the balustrade, he rolled the tension from his neck.

For so many years he'd wished his mother dead. It had been a wish he'd hated himself for but one he'd been unable to block. Not until he'd learned she'd been dead for four days before her body had been found had he recognised the miserable loneliness of her death had been a mirror to the miserable loneliness of her life.

The grief he'd felt at her death had knocked him for six. How had Marisa described grief? Like swimming through a black cloud?

His had been a grief he'd never expected to feel and he'd hated himself for it. She'd never grieved for the loss of him so why should he grieve for the loss of her? He'd smothered the grief quickly and locked it away. Forgotten.

Until now.

He waited until the tight knots deep in his guts had loosened before returning to Marisa's room.

The knots loosened some more to see his son sitting on the bed, wide awake. A huge beam spread over Niki's face to see him.

Nikos met Marisa's eyes.

She shrugged ruefully. 'He's not used to sleeping in new places. This is only the second time he's not slept in his own cot. We spent a night in Geneva when the cartel was being taken down—I think he woke up four times.'

Niki held his arms out for him. Nikos slid under the bedsheets and pulled his son to him. If Marisa still wanted him to leave she'd have to ask again.

But she didn't ask. She slipped under the sheets next to him and smiled to see their son bouncing on Nikos's chest.

'He loves you,' she observed, her wistful gaze alternating between his face and their son's.

'I like to think so.'

'He does.' Lightly—so lightly it felt like a feather brushing against him—she ran a finger over his forehead then turned her attention to their son, whose cheek she kissed. Her shoulders rose before she let out a long sigh and lay down.

Pulling the covers over her shoulders, she said, 'If you snore, you go back to your own room.'

His chest had filled with too much emotion for him to protest at this slight with anything stronger than, 'I don't snore.'

The sad amusement in her eyes filled his chest even more. 'Don't let him stay awake too long otherwise we'll have a grumpy baby tomorrow.'

He swallowed the boulder lodged in his throat and nodded. 'Understood.'

Her eyes held his for the blink of a moment before she turned her back to him and turned the light out.

Struggling to breathe, Nikos held his son's wrists to steady him as he merrily bounced away on his chest and watched his happy, babbling face in the starlight.

'Nikos?' Marisa's sleepy voice broke quietly through the darkness. 'We'll talk more about your suggestion tomorrow. Okay?'

# CHAPTER TEN

NEVER IN HIS life had Nikos woken with such a weight pressing on his chest. But this was a good weight. An excellent weight. He opened his eyes and found his son straddling his neck, his face hovering over his with the look of an archaeologist examining an important find. The sun had risen but Nikos was quite sure it was earlier than he'd woken since his own childhood.

Grinning, he lifted Niki into the air and sat up, shushing him as he went so he didn't wake Marisa, who was curled up like a hedgehog under the sheets beside him.

He stared at the golden-red curls poking out and felt his heart catch. On the verge of leaning over and capturing one of those curls, he was prevented by a miniature finger being inserted up his nose.

He held onto his laughter until he'd closed the nursery door. His amusement soon turned to head-scratching as he tasked himself with cleaning and changing his son's nappy and pyjamas. Just as he was debating whether or not to wake the nanny, a sleepy

Marisa entered the room, smothering a yawn. Even with her hair shooting up in all directions and puffy eyed, she looked beautiful, and Nikos felt an immediate stab of longing pierce him.

He'd hardly slept himself. While his son and son's mother had slept deeply with him on the huge emperor-sized bed, he'd been alert to every move they'd both made, the few lulls into sleep filled with vivid dreams that had merged into reality when he'd opened his eyes.

Had his mother ever brought him into her bed when he'd been a baby? Had his father? Had they ever shared the same room? All he'd ever known was that each had had their own room that the other was expressly forbidden from entering. He'd been forbidden from entering either of them too. He remembered mornings, his stomach hurting from hunger, creeping around the vast kitchen in search of food, dragging a stool around to climb on to reach the taller cupboards, too frightened of their anger to go into their rooms to wake either of them for help. Neither had minded him making a mess in the kitchen—his mess only added to theirs—but woe betide him if he woke them up. Those were the only rules in the Manolas household: no entering his parents' bedrooms and no making a noise that could wake them from their sleep.

When he'd first been taken from them he'd thought it was because he'd made too much early morning noise. It had taken a long time to realise that, though he'd been forcibly taken, they'd willingly let him go. They'd given him up.

What had been so wrong with him that they could do that? Give him up? It was a question he'd asked himself many times through the years but it took on an even greater significance now.

What had been so wrong with him that they'd denied him the affection Marisa lavished on Niki? Look at her now, standing beside him at the changing table, pressing kisses on the face of their naked son, who was making bicycle motions with his legs. He didn't imagine his mother had ever done that to him.

'Why didn't you wake me?' she asked.

'When did you last sleep in?' he challenged.

'What's sleeping in?'

'See?' He gave her his sternest look. 'Go back to bed. I've got this.'

Ignoring his directive, she tickled their son's belly. 'You're changing him?'

'Obviously.'

'If it's that obvious, where's his clean clothes?'

He hadn't thought of that. From the look on her face, she knew it too. She smiled. 'I'll get some for you. Shall I get you a clean nappy too?'

He hadn't thought about that either.

He had a lot to learn. From the look on Marisa's face she was happy and willing to teach him.

He just had to hope she was happy and willing to teach him as his wife.

The first full day in Mykonos passed slowly for Marisa. Spent lazing around the pool with the nanny and Stratos, who still seemed to be cold towards her, it gave her plenty of thinking time. All her thoughts were wrapped around Nikos…

The lovemaking they'd shared. That was something she didn't so much think about but shimmered in her veins as a constant reminder. Her pride wanted to be angry that his seduction had been planned but she'd waited for him on that balcony. She'd wanted it as much as he had and from the ache in her pelvis, she knew that if he came to her room tonight, she would open the door to him without hesitation.

Making love had been a physical act she'd abandoned herself to without fear of losing her heart. The feelings that had erupted within her when he'd spoken so dispassionately about his childhood were far more frightening. She'd felt the pieces of her damaged heart knit themselves back together so they could cry with sympathy for the damaged little boy he'd been. The Nikos he was today was not the six-year-old child he'd once been, and it was imperative she separate those two Nikoses, however difficult it would be, especially if she agreed to his proposal.

That, more than anything, had played on her mind all day, tying all the other issues together and making the strings of her heart play a concerto.

Terrifyingly, she had slept more soundly with him sharing her bed than she had since the day he'd gone missing from his yacht. Today was the first morning since his return that she hadn't woken with panicked ice stabbing her heart.

She genuinely didn't know what to do for the best. Could she really deny her son the opportunity to have the blessed childhood she'd had for the sake of her pride? And could she deny Nikos that experience? Didn't he deserve the chance to be a real father, to share in all the joys of watching their baby reach all those important milestones and all the day-to-day joys she took for granted? The joy of beaming early morning smiles? The joy of feeding him something that wasn't immediately spat out? The joy of baths and getting drenched by manically kicking legs connecting to water?

She had to wait until mid-afternoon before the opportunity came to ask Nikos the questions that had been steadily forming in her jumbled mind as the day had gone on. His grandfather had gone to his chess club and the nanny had taken Niki to the nursery for his nap.

Nikos joined her on the terrace, a smile on his gorgeous face and two glasses of fruity cocktails in his hands.

'Here,' he said, handing her one. 'Don't worry, it's not too strong.'

The strings of her heart were plucked again. How well he was getting to know her as a mother, anticipating her thoughts and worries.

There was something incredible in how he could make the separation of her as a mother and her as a woman and cater for the needs of both. More incredible still that it had taken his return for her needs as a woman to reawaken.

He'd roused so many buried feelings and impulses. Feelings and impulses he'd been the one to bring to life in the first place...

'Thank you,' she murmured. This was the first time they'd been alone together all day and, from the safety of her shades, she let her greedy eyes soak in the glory of his body, only a pair of brief black swim shorts covering any flesh. She'd always loved his body. Its muscular leanness. The olive hue of his skin. The dark hair that covered his chest and made a tapering line down to his groin. The snake hips. The tight buttocks. The long, toned legs. The whole package.

From the smirk on his face and the way he brushed his fingers against hers as he released the cocktail glass, Nikos knew exactly what she was doing. She didn't care that she'd been caught ogling him. After the night they'd shared and the confidences he'd entrusted to her, she was beyond denying her desire for him. It was too late for denial. Much too late.

Propping herself on an elbow to face him, she had a sip of the cocktail while he stretched out on the sunbed placed inches from hers, and felt heat crawl over her face as his eyes, also hidden by shades, swept over the length of *her* swimsuit-clad form.

'Your body's changed,' she said. 'You're more muscular.'

He grinned. 'I lived in a log cabin in the Alaskan Mountains for eighteen months. If I wanted heat, I had to chop trees for firewood. Trust me, in the winter months it gets *very* cold.'

About to ask about his time in exile, her words

were stolen when he extended a hand and encircled one of her breasts. 'Your body's changed too.'

She shivered at his touch and put her glass on the table at the top of the adjoining sunbeds. 'Having a baby does that to a woman.'

He smiled knowingly and rubbed his thumb over a nipple. 'Having a baby has only made you more beautiful.'

She couldn't help her snort of derision at this.

He caught a curl in his fingers. 'Why do you find that funny?'

'You haven't seen me naked in the light yet.'

*'Yet?'* He quirked his eyebrows. 'Then I have something to look forward to?'

'Maybe.'

He put his head in the crook of his elbow and inched his face closer to her. 'There is no one here now...'

She put a finger to his lips without thinking. He kissed it.

'Nikos...' She sighed.

He rubbed the tip of his nose to hers. 'Yes, *agapi mou*?'

The warmth of his breath seeped into her pores and it took more effort than she would have believed possible to keep her thoughts on track. 'What we were talking about last night... Your idea of marriage.'

He rubbed his nose against her cheek. 'Have you decided it's an excellent idea?'

She moved away a little and rolled onto her back

but that attempt at distance did nothing to stop his hands roaming over her body. Pressing her thighs tightly together, she tried to tune out the sensations skipping over her skin at his touch. 'If I'm going to agree to it, we would have to live in Valencia.'

'I know.'

'I know Mykonos is your home but it's too far from the business and too far from my family. My mama loves Niki. She's been the most wonderful support to me. I can't take him from her.'

He made slow circles around a hard nipple with his finger. 'I've already agreed to that, *agapi mou*.'

'Oh.' She swallowed. She should slap his hand away but it felt too good. 'So you have. Sorry.' She had to swallow the moisture filling her mouth again. 'I was so prepared and ready with arguments that I didn't listen properly to your answer.'

His fingers dragged down her belly. 'I would want us to spend a good amount of time here too,' he told her as he gently cupped her pubis. 'I want Niki to know this as his home too. But I agree, it is more practical for us to make Valencia our main home.'

His fingers drifted away from her as he rose to his feet. He pinched the sides of his shorts and fixed his hooded eyes on her. She hadn't even noticed him remove his shades. 'Anything else?'

He tugged his shorts down. His enormous erection sprang free.

She could hardly think, never mind speak through the lust rampaging through her. 'I want Niki to go to school in Valencia.'

He sat on the edge of her sunbed and pulled the straps of her swimsuit down. 'He is too young for us to worry about school yet. We can decide that nearer the time.'

'And…' He'd pulled the top of her swimsuit past her breasts and immediately taken one in his mouth while he slowly pulled the rest of the suit down.

'Yes, *agapi mou*?'

'No…taking…' She squeezed her eyes shut and tried to concentrate, even though he'd tugged the swimsuit down past her thighs. Only dimly did she realise she'd actively helped him in removing it and that it was her kicking the suit away.

He climbed between her legs and gazed down at her. 'No taking…?'

'Charge,' she breathed.

'Like this?' He slid inside her, long, deep, all the way to the hilt. Then, before she could really savour the sensation, immediately pulled out. 'No taking charge like that?'

'Nikos…' His name sounded like a moan from her lips.

He plunged inside her again. 'Is that what you meant?'

He made to pull out of her again. She grabbed hold of his buttocks with both hands to keep him in place.

'You win,' she breathed, wrapping her legs tightly around him. 'Take charge.'

'And you'll marry me?'

'*Yes.*' At that moment she would have agreed to anything to stop him pulling out of her again.

'Then I take charge with pleasure.'

'Time to get up.'

Marisa opened a bleary eye and found Nikos perched on the edge of the bed beside her. 'What time is it?'

'Nine.'

She lifted her head. A cup of coffee had been placed on her bedside table beside the baby monitor. 'Why didn't you wake me?'

'Because you're adorable when you sleep.' He placed his lips to her ear and whispered, 'If our son hadn't woken so early, I would have woken you in a much more pleasurable manner.'

She found it incredible that she'd slept so late *and* slept through the early morning babbling she'd always been so attuned to. Either she'd been exhausted from making love until the early hours or her subconscious had let her sleep soundly, knowing Nikos was taking care of their son. The latter, she decided as she tilted her head for a kiss and breathed in his freshly showered and shaved scent.

'Where is he?'

'With Seema in the nursery. And you need to get up. We have an appointment to attend.'

'Have we?'

He kissed her mouth. 'Yes, *agapi mou*. An appointment to register our intention to marry. We can book the wedding too. Get everything in hand.'

The last of her sleepiness flew away. Sitting upright, she stared at him. 'Since when are we getting married?'

'You agreed to it yesterday.'

So she had. Under sexual duress. After she'd said yes, they'd made love hard and fast on the sunbed then gone to bed and made love at a much more leisurely pace until Niki had woken from his nap. The early evening had been spent with their son and then, the minute he was asleep, they'd gone straight back to bed.

Truth was, they'd been far too busy talking with their bodies to speak verbally.

Truth was, she'd happily shoved her agreement to marry him to the back of her mind rather than confront the magnitude of what she'd done, and now that she was confronted with it, darts of panic were making their way through her.

'I didn't agree to marry you immediately.'

'The decision has been made so why wait?'

*Because you don't love me!*

Love? Since when had she started thinking about Nikos along those lines again? She didn't love *him*. She loved their son and she wanted him to have the same happy childhood she'd had, and Nikos deserved to be a father to him every bit as much as she was a mother to him. He'd hurt her badly, something she would never forget, but now she understood him better, she was prepared to move on from that hurt for their son's sake. Hadn't Nikos proved he deserved that chance? He'd swiftly bought into the business, installed his top people to assist her and take the load off her—she wouldn't be here in Mykonos now if he hadn't done that—and he'd proved his devotion to their son. *Those* were the reasons she'd agreed to marry him. She'd been prepared to marry Raul for the business and Niki's sake, so why not marry Niki's actual father? The damage he'd inflicted had been too great for him to hurt her again but the passion between them was every bit as strong as it had always been. At least marrying Nikos meant marrying a man she was happy to share a bed with!

What she must not do, under any circumstance, was think about Nikos as a child in desperate need of someone to love and care for him, and think she could be the woman to do that.

'I agreed on the proviso you didn't take charge,' she said.

He raised a brow, the look in his eyes as he brought his face to hers making her pelvis contract. 'Really? Because I seem to remember you *begging* me to take charge.'

She leaned into him, her lips tingling from the whispered heat of his breath...

'You're not doing this again.' She darted away from him and jumped off the bed, hurrying to the far wall.

'Doing what again?'

'Using your magic penis to stop me thinking properly.'

The look he gave her was one of incredulousness.

And then his gorgeous face broke into a grin and he burst into a deep rumble of laughter.

Nikos laughed so long and so hard his chest hurt. 'I have a magic penis?' He chortled, wiping mirth-induced tears from his eyes.

Eyes alight with amusement, she sniggered. 'Why else do you think I agreed to marry you?'

He got to his feet.

She shot a hand out in warning. 'Stay back. Do not touch me until we've discussed this.'

He loved a challenge. Especially when given by a sexy, sleep-tousled redhead who thought he had a magic penis.

'I want to marry in Spain.'

Locking his gaze on her, he took a step towards her. 'Why?'

'That's where my family are.'

He took another step. 'They can fly here. I want to marry here on Mykonos.'

'Why?'

*Because I can marry you quickly here, and the sooner I marry you, the sooner I know my rights as a father are protected. The less time I give you to think about it, the less time you have to change your mind.*

He took her extended hand and pinned it above her head, staring deep into the lust-riven dark eyes. 'We have better beaches.'

He cut her protest away with a kiss.

# CHAPTER ELEVEN

Marisa was adding blusher to her cheeks when Nikos walked into her bedroom. Her heart thumped to see him and she had to concentrate hard to affect nonchalance at his appearance and stop her hand from reacting to the thump and splodging blusher over her nose.

After they'd made the wedding arrangements that morning, Nikos had casually mentioned they would be going to his nightclub on the island that night to celebrate their engagement.

She'd been unable to think of one good reason to refuse.

Not having bothered to pack any going-out clothes, she'd got him to drop her at the main shopping district in Chora so she could buy herself an outfit to party in. She'd wandered through designer boutiques and more touristy shops with no idea why the thought of celebrating made her feel so bereft.

She'd agreed to marry him. She'd agreed it would happen in Mykonos. She'd agreed it would happen this coming weekend. She didn't have a clue how he'd got the officials to agree for it to happen so quickly, but here she was, a day after she'd told him one of her terms for agreeing to marriage was that he had to stop taking charge, just five days from actually doing the deed.

To make the day extra special, they would be marrying on their son's first birthday. She thought this fitting. The stars were aligning to approve her decision.

On top of all that, Nikos had agreed to her stipulation about them living in Spain. So what did she have to feel bereft about?

And why had she found herself wandering away from the shops and into the more residential areas with the strings of her heart tugging manically to imagine a small Nikos playing on the uneven cobbled streets?

He walked over to where she sat at the dressing table, lifted her hair and placed a kiss to the nape of her neck. Sensation quivered deliciously over her skin.

'You smell gorgeous,' he murmured, 'and look spectacular.'

She met his reflection in the mirror and smiled through the ache growing in her chest. He looked pretty spectacular himself. Dressed in black chinos, dark grey shirt unbuttoned at the throat and a charcoal blazer, he managed to look smart, casual, elegant and devilishly handsome all at once.

'Did you get hold of your mother?' he asked.

She nodded as she opened her palate of eyeshadow.

'And?'

'She said to tell you that if you hurt me, she'll personally see that you never father another child.'

There was a flickering in his eyes but his tone remained casual. 'And what did you say to that?'

'That I'm not stupid enough to let you hurt me again.' She picked up a brush and dabbed it into the glittering deep brown colour and met his gaze again before applying it to her eyelids. 'Our marriage is for Niki's sake. We both know that. And now she knows that.'

'But is she supportive of it?'

'Yes.'

'And your sister?'

'She thinks I'm mad, but she's coming to the wedding.'

'Why does she think you're mad?'

She shrugged, taking a fresh brush and dabbing it into the glittering gold colour. She wouldn't repeat her sister's furious rant about Marisa throwing her life away on a man who'd happily discarded her like unwanted trash. But Elsa wasn't a mother with a child who would thrive much better with his father a permanent part of his life. 'Elsa's in love. She thinks only people in love should marry.'

'And what do you think?'

'That love marriages are, historically speaking, a recent thing.' She reached for her mascara. 'History is littered with successful marriages built without love.' And she'd spent an hour sitting on the beach terrace of his nightclub, which was a café by day, searching her phone for examples of them while waiting for Nikos to collect her.

'I bet those successful marriages had great sex at their core.'

'But only with each other.' She held his gaze a moment longer before applying her mascara, trying her hardest to keep her hand steady so she didn't poke herself in the eye at the lie she'd just uttered.

Most of the successful non-love marriages she'd read about had only been successful because both spouses had either turned a blind eye to other lovers or explicitly agreed to them.

She knew there was no way she could tolerate or accept infidelity—just the thought of Nikos in the arms of another woman made her stomach churn violently—and had searched even harder for the faithful marriages. But those had brought no comfort either. They had been successful because the couples had fallen in love with each other.

Nikos heard the unspoken warning and put his hands on her shoulders to drop a kiss into her hair. 'Then I am ahead of you on this one,' he said silkily. 'There has been only you since the day we met and while you wear this, there will be only you.'

She twisted to face him.

He dug into his back pocket and pulled out a black velvet box. He flicked the lid open and held it out to her. 'Your engagement ring.'

She stared at it for the longest time. He wondered if she was waiting for him to drop to one knee. That, of course, would be ludicrous.

Strangely, when he'd found the ring—and he'd scoured every jewellery shop in Chora before finding his gaze drawn to this one—he'd examined it closely with an unbidden fantasy playing out in his mind. In that fantasy he'd dropped to one knee. In that fantasy, Marisa had cupped her cheeks in delight then thrown her arms around him. In that fantasy, she'd said she loved him.

He'd pulled himself out of the fantasy with his guts twisting. They twisted now to remember it. It had to be fatherhood causing this unseemly sentimentality. Nikos's love for his son was like a garden of drab weeds suddenly filled with beautifully scented colourful flowers. It was not unreasonable to suppose his subconscious would try to extend that love to the mother of his son.

'Are you going to try it on?' he asked when she made no move to touch the ring.

She plucked it from the box and slid it on her wedding finger. Then she got to her feet and held it out to him. 'It's perfect.'

For a moment he was too taken with the whole effect to respond. Wearing a short black sequined wrap-around dress that hugged her curves and exposed just the right amount of cleavage, she glittered; an exotic shimmering mirage. She must have sprayed something in her hair too for, under the ceiling light, it glimmered too.

At that moment, all he could think was that *she* was perfect.

* * *

Stratos, who'd taken his lady friend out to dinner, was getting out of his car as Marisa slipped into the back of Nikos's. She waved. The lady friend waved back. Stratos pretended not to see her.

'Why does your grandfather hate me?' she asked Nikos when his driver set off.

'He doesn't hate you.'

'Haven't you noticed? He barely acknowledges my existence.'

After a moment, he sighed. 'He is angry you didn't tell him about Niki.'

She tried to keep her composure but his unexpected answer pierced straight through her.

'Why didn't you tell him?' The question was asked amiably enough but she could see the curiosity in the light brown eyes.

'Nikos…' About to tell him how she'd fallen to pieces when he'd been presumed dead, she stopped herself. 'Your death… I was grieving you when I learned I was pregnant.' It had suddenly struck her, the only moment of clarity in two weeks of desolation and anguish, that her daily bouts of nausea might have a different cause to grief: The food poisoning she'd suffered the month before his disappearance and the realisation it could have affected the contraceptive pill she took faithfully.

Had she blocked out the effects it could have on the pill because she'd subconsciously *wanted* a baby…?

Shaking off the ridiculous thought, she said, 'The

pregnancy came as a shock…' The biggest shock but also the most miraculous. 'But a good shock.' Good enough to pull her out of the pit of despair and give her focus.

His eyes bored into her. 'You were glad to be carrying my child?'

She touched the tips of her fingers to his warm cheek. 'Knowing I had your child growing inside me gave me more comfort than you can imagine. I never intended to keep it a secret, I just wanted to get past the three-month mark before I told anyone other than my immediate family. I guess I was being superstitious about it but the fear of miscarrying was very real to me.' Terrifying.

Even now she dreaded to think what she would have done if she'd lost her baby, lost that last link to Nikos in those dark times.

'But then, when I reached the safe three-month mark, all the stuff with the cartel started. I found Rocco dead…' She closed her eyes to clear the image of her beautiful dog, drowned in the pool. 'I cannot tell you how frightened I was. I was terrified they'd learn about the pregnancy. By the time Niki was born, I'd lost my father to the cartel too and my life had turned into a nightmare. All I cared about—and I do mean *all*—was keeping him safe and protected from them. We turned the estate into a fortress that I hid our son and myself in as much as I could.'

Marisa watched Nikos as she spoke, watched as his face slowly tightened into stillness, his only reaction an almost imperceptible movement of his Adam's apple.

'I'm sorry I didn't reach out to your grandfather,' she whispered. 'I should have done. I should have thought of him, and if I'd known how close you were and just how much he meant to you, I would have done. Please, tell him it wasn't deliberate malice on my part and that I'm really sorry I hurt him.'

Lips taut, he bowed his head. 'I will explain everything to him.'

'Thank you.'

Nikos rested his head back and blew out a long breath of air, fighting the cauldron of emotions battering his guts at all she'd had to deal with.

He should have been there.

'You remember the day you first saw me with Niki?' she said, breaking through his thoughts.

He pinched the bridge of his nose and nodded.

'That was the first time he'd left the estate since he was born. I had him at home,' she added.

'That explains why he's so shy with strangers,' he said, attempting a smile.

'Probably.' She covered his hand with hers and gently squeezed.

'I did wonder why you hid yourself away even before your father's death,' he mused aloud, returning the caress.

Her face jerked. 'What are you talking about?'

'I had you watched,' he admitted.

Her eyes widened in shock.

'The cartel sent me a photo of you,' he reminded

her, speaking evenly to fight the bile that always rose whenever he remembered the moment Marisa's picture had suddenly appeared amongst the photos of his lawyer's desecrated body.

Nikos had already been fighting a roll of nausea but that picture of Marisa, clearly taken using a long-range lens, had pushed him over the edge and he'd vomited for the first time in his adult life.

'Felipe Lorenzi's team helped me fake my death and protect my people, and I paid them to put a team together to watch over you too.'

Even beneath the make-up she wore, colour stained her face.

'I had them keep watch over the estate and follow you closely but discreetly every time you left it, and report to me daily by email. I did the same with my grandfather.' He managed a smile. 'Wi-Fi was practically the only modern convenience that log cabin had. I needed to assure myself that you were safe. My biggest regret is that I didn't ask them to watch your whole family as well when they left the estate.' He swallowed back another wave of nausea. 'I didn't know your family had been dealing with the cartel too, not until after your father's death.'

She continued to stare at him. He could see her thinking, putting all the pieces of the puzzle together. When she spoke, a tremor rang through her voice. 'So, when we employed Felipe to fortify our home with his men and to work with us and the international security services to bring the cartel down, they were already working for you on the same thing?'

He inclined his head.

'Then how did you not know about our son?'

'For reasons of confidentiality.' Nikos had confronted Felipe about his failure to mention in a single one of his staff's reports about Marisa, the pregnancy or subsequent birth of Niki. 'My instructions were to keep a watchful eye on you and to take action at any sign of danger. When your family then came to employ his team too, they were bound under strict privacy contracts. Would you have welcomed them into your home and entrusted your physical safety to them if you'd thought they would discuss your private lives with others?'

Lips clamped together, she hesitated then shook her head.

'If the pregnancy or Niki's birth had been relevant to any of the reports, I would have been told, but the subject never came up. God knows, I wish it had…'

'Would it have changed things if you had known about him?' she asked.

'I don't know.' He clamped his jaws together. 'Maybe it was for the best that I didn't know. If I'd reappeared before they were taken down you would have been an even bigger target for them. But those months… Marisa, they were the hardest of my life. Physically. Mentally. When I learned the cartel had targeted your family, I thought I was going mad. The only thing that stopped me—'

He cut himself off, thrown back again to the sheer terror that had clutched his heart and how close he'd come to hiking through the mountains to get to civilisation and back to her.

He took a deep breath and continued. 'Once I knew Felipe had taken responsibility for your family's safety I could think a little straighter but it was still hard. I hate to think I would have endangered you or our son for the sake of my ego.'

'It must have been hard for you being so far from the action and for all that time,' Marisa intuited. Nikos was such a take-charge man she could imagine nothing more excruciating for him than being stuck thousands of kilometres away, unable to influence anything.

'It was horrendous. Felipe must have known I would struggle to be so far from you…from everything…and that's why I was given a log cabin in the middle of nowhere that needed constant maintenance.' He managed a grin. 'It's hard to spend your days brooding when there's trees to fell and water to collect if you want to drink or clean yourself.'

Oh, God, tears were forming. Marisa could feel them stabbing into her eyes and she blinked rapidly to stop them falling, using her hand as a fan to dry them.

'What's wrong?' he asked.

She smiled to assure him she was fine but didn't dare open her mouth, not until she had control of herself.

The deprivation he'd put himself through. The isolation.

Eighteen months of his life.

She'd never thought of it in those terms before or

considered how tough it must have been for such a gregarious man to give up everything that made life a joy and hide in the shadows, or considered how selfless his actions had been.

He'd done all that, in part, for her. And he'd paid for her to be watched over. He hadn't just faked his death and forgotten about her, as she'd thought, he'd paid a crack team of ex-special forces to watch over her and keep her safe, long before she'd even known the murderous cartel existed.

Did that mean that he *had* cared for her?

But if he had, then why had he, before he'd discovered their son's existence, been happy for her to learn of his resurrection on the grapevine? If you cared for someone, you didn't treat them like that.

Could things be any more confusing?

As she fanned her hand in front of her face, her engagement ring glinted. It was an art deco style, pear-cut champagne diamond set in rose-gold. When he'd produced it, she'd had to work so hard not to let the joy burst out of her.

Marisa absolutely adored champagne diamonds. Loved the colours and the way they changed under the light. And she loved rose-gold over normal gold. And she loved anything art deco.

The man who wanted to marry her so he could always be a part of their son's life had given her the engagement ring of her dreams.

The driver stopped outside a typical Mykonos building; whitewashed Cycladic style, set along a narrow

cobbled street but which differed from the other bus-
tling streets they'd driven through by the sheer number of people queuing like overdressed bunches of
grapes for admission. It was all very different from
when she'd waited for him earlier, drinking coffee
on the club's beach terrace.

When she stepped out of the car, the flash of cam-
eras in Marisa's face announced the paparazzi's presence.

In an instant, Nikos was at her side, taking her
hand and sweeping her past the enormous bouncers, who parted in surprisingly nimble fashion to
admit them.

Inside, the feel and vibe of the place were exactly
what she expected from her experiences at his other
nightclubs. Bodies packed like sardines, drinks in
hand, swaying under multi-coloured strobe lights
to the pumping beat. A Manolas nightclub was not
somewhere you went for conversation. It was a place
you went to dance the night away to the best DJs in
the world.

The VIP section of his Mykonos club was reached
by a set of wide stairs that formed a semi-circle
around the main dance floor. More bouncers guarded
the entrance to it. One unhooked the red tasselled
rope barrier and nodded a respectful greeting as they
slipped past them.

The inner sanctum was far less crowded than the
ground floor and she recognised many of the faces
in it even if she didn't know them personally. They
all seemed to know her, though, or *of* her, and as she

sipped champagne, flashed her engagement ring at anyone who asked, and had shouted conversation with one of Nikos's cousins, she relaxed.

She'd always relaxed in Nikos's clubs. In her university years she'd often gone on girls' weekends away to Ibiza and always they had dressed up and hit Manolas. They'd all agreed it was their favourite club because they felt safe there. Plentiful bouncers and more discreet undercover security in the crowds had stopped drunken wandering hands going too far, and then there had been the freedom of knowing your drink wouldn't get spiked thanks to the strict no-drugs policy. Having your bags searched and having to empty your pockets at the entrance was a small price to pay for that kind of safety.

It had never occurred to her to question why Nikos enforced such a tough policy on drugs, not even when they'd formed a relationship, and, as she cast her gaze around the heaving dance floor, she thought again of everything it had cost him to stop the cartel from filling this place and all his other clubs with their narcotics and help stop anyone else falling into the kind of addiction that had turned his parents into monsters and ultimately killed his mother.

'What are you thinking?' he asked, speaking into her ear to be heard.

She smiled and rose up on her toes to plant a kiss to his mouth. That was something he often asked. If he didn't care for her, why would he want to know?

As the night went on and the partying got more raucous and Nikos stayed glued to her side, she found herself asking the same questions—if Nikos really only wanted to marry her for their son's sake, why did he care so much about what she thought? Why had he gone out of his way to choose the perfect engagement ring for her?

And, if he didn't care for her, why had he gone to so much effort to keep her safe even before he'd known their son existed?

'Let's get some air,' she shouted after the midnight hour had struck.

Hands clasped, they headed out to the huge VIP terrace.

Avoiding the smoking section, they settled on a secluded sweetheart seat and let the sea breeze cool their skin. Outside, the noise levels were far more favourable for conversation but Marisa was content to listen to the laughter from the revellers on the ground floor beach terrace and the snatched chatter of others partying on their own.

Fingers playing absently with the buttons of his shirt, she only realised she'd undone one and had slipped her hand under it to encircle a nipple when he huskily said, 'What are you doing?'

'Touching you.' She tilted her head to stare into his eyes. 'Do you want me to stop?'

His eyes gleamed. 'No.'

'Good.' She stretched her leg and then casually hooked it over his lap. A large hand rested on her thigh, right at the hem that had ruched up to skim her bottom. Marisa leaned into him and pressed her face into his neck. 'You smell amazing.'

Moving her hand from his nipple, she pulled it out from beneath his shirt and slowly trailed her fingers down his stomach to his belt.

When her fingers gently traced over the length of his erection, straining beneath the confines of his chinos, Nikos tightened the grip on his glass of bourbon. There was something incredibly seductive about her touch and the way she kept nuzzling her nose into his neck, arousing him despite the revellers spilling out in all directions.

How far was she prepared to take this?

How far was he prepared to let her take it?

She lifted her face to lick the lobe of his ear. 'I haven't thanked you properly for my ring, have I?'

She gently cupped his erection again before her fingers crept back up his chest. He didn't know if he was relieved or disappointed, then found himself swallowing as she moved her thigh just enough that her knee pressed against his excitement.

'When we get back, I'll thank you properly,' she breathed, rubbing her nose over his cheek then capturing his bottom lip with her teeth. She nipped it gently at the same moment she encircled his other nipple.

He tightened his grip on her thigh, fighting the heady urge to slip his fingers beneath the material.

Just at the moment lust was about to override propriety, she unhooked her leg, jumped to her feet and tugged at his hand. 'That's enough air. Let's dance.'

Stunned at the change of pace, he stared at the

beautiful face alive with more delight than he had seen in…since he'd come back to her.

'You want to dance?' he managed to croak.

She pulled her lips together before another wide smile lit her face, and she leaned over to speak in his ear, giving him a wonderful view of her naked breasts in the dip made in the material. 'Not really. I want you to take me home.'

He just stared at her. Somehow, her smile widened even more.

'Have I stopped you thinking, *mi amado*?' Wickedness flashed in her eyes before she slipped her hand over his buttocks and ran her tongue over his lips. 'Now you know how you make *me* feel.'

Then she stepped back again and waved the phone he hadn't even felt her filch from his back pocket at him.

Nikos snatched it from her and called his driver.

## CHAPTER TWELVE

THE MOMENT THEY were alone in the private cabin of his car, Nikos turned off the microphone connecting them to the driver and pulled Marisa in for a kiss he'd thought he might explode from waiting for.

Whatever burning arousal her teasing had done to him, it had had the same effect on her. In a medley of tongues and ferociously moving lips, she straddled him, her hands going straight to the buttons of his shirt and practically ripping them apart. At his waist, she yanked on his belt and then, with a grace that was almost poetic, she dropped to her knees on the cabin's spacious floor. Undoing his chinos, she grasped the sides and tugged them down past his hips and then, finally, freed him from the torturous confines.

There was no hesitation. Her head dipped and she took him in her mouth.

*Theos*, but the sensations were incredible. Mindblowing. The way she ran her tongue the length of it, the way she squeezed...

He groaned and closed his eyes, reaching for her hair to thread his fingers through.

What was it about this woman he reacted to so viscerally? How did her touch burn him in a way that no one else's did?

When she danced back up his body to straddle him again, he clasped the back of her head and kissed her deeply, a kiss broken as he moaned into her mouth at the encompassing pleasure that filled him as she sank down on him.

The relief of having Nikos inside her was so great that Marisa held onto it for as long as she could. Already there was a quickening building inside her and she tried her hardest to fight it, wanting to savour the pleasure.

Then, as she finally began to ride him, throwing her head back in ecstasy when his mouth closed over an aching nipple, she realised this was a pleasure she would enjoy for the rest of her life and, bucking onto him, she cried out the rapture erupting through her every pore.

Marisa lay with her head on Nikos's chest, listening to his heartbeat. She loved the solid thump it made against her cheek, the way it seemed to sink through her skin and become a part of her.

'Are you awake?' she whispered.

It had to be at least three in the morning. After their frantic drive home, they'd rushed through the villa to his bedroom and done it all again. She should be shattered but she was still buzzing from the adrenaline of the best night out she'd had in possibly for ever.

'That depends on what you want,' he murmured sleepily, tightening his hold around her.

'Nothing. Well, nothing for a few more minutes,' she teased.

Stroking her back, he laughed. 'I think I might need a few more minutes too, *agapi mou*.'

She gently nipped at a flat, brown nipple.

'You're sex mad.' There was admiration in his voice.

'Sex mad for *you*,' she corrected.

'As long as it's only for me then carry on.'

She dragged herself over his chest so her breasts crushed against it and she could look at his gorgeous face. 'You do know it is only you, don't you?'

A furrow formed in his brow.

She kissed him lightly and ran her fingers through his hair, then sighed dreamily. 'You're the only man I've ever wanted, the only man I've ever been with and the only man I'll ever be with.'

Suddenly she was flat on her back, Nikos pinning her to the mattress as he stared into her eyes, the expression on his face unreadable before he suddenly crushed his mouth to hers in a kiss so passionately violent that arousal flared for them both again and soon Marisa was moaning in his arms and clinging to him as he drove their mutual passion to glorious heights.

The next few days managed to pass both crazily fast and crazily slow. On the one hand was their forthcoming wedding, the reception of which was doubling as a birthday party for their son. Everything had been booked and guests confirmed. Nikos had employed the most efficient wedding planner and given her all the funds needed to grease any palms that needed it. The day seemed to be approaching with the speed of a freight train.

The crazily slow side came from the joy of just being alive. Nikos's grandfather had gone away on a trip for a few days with his lady friend, which helped Marisa relax around the villa. Many happy hours were spent with Nikos and their son, just the three of them. In the evenings they would put Niki to bed and when Marisa was satisfied he was fast asleep, they would lock the bedroom door and make love until they were so spent that sleep claimed them, whether they wanted it to or not.

After three days of this bliss, Nikos went to his business centre to catch up on neglected work. With her own business being taken care of and nothing of any urgency needing her attention, Marisa left Niki napping under the watchful eye of his nanny and set off with the butler to decide where to house her family and the other guests who would be staying with them for the wedding.

The guest villas, she decided, were the best place for her friends, who could be as loud as they liked without disturbing anyone, and she pointed to their names on Angelos's clipboard, trying out a little Greek on him. He beamed and congratulated her efforts, which in turn made her beam with pride.

She'd asked Seema to speak to her in Greek when they were alone in an effort to speed up her understanding of the language. Soon, she hoped to surprise Nikos by conversing with him in his native tongue.

With the guest villas allocated, they returned to the main villa.

Marisa had never been on the second floor before and she found the rooms as spacious and richly furnished as those on the first floor, all except for one room. That room had only a large, battered ottoman in it.

Once the rest of the guests had been assigned their rooms and Angelos had gone back downstairs, curiosity took her back to the unfurnished room.

It was just an ordinary room with white walls, duck egg blue drapes and a soft grey carpet. All the same, she found herself hesitating before entering it and walking to the ottoman.

She crouched down and lifted the lid. Her nose wrinkled at the stale, musty scent that was released. Within the ottoman's confines was a jumble of toys.

Her heart lurched. These were the last things she'd expected to find.

Cautiously, she picked up a ragged stuffed elephant and ran her finger over the indentation made by a missing eye. There were more stuffed toys, plastic army figures, children's jigsaws, plastic trucks and other assorted toys crammed inside. Everything looked old. Faded. Forgotten.

She turned at the sound of approaching footsteps and then Nikos appeared with Niki in his arms.

There was the strangest expression on his face, one that immediately made her think she'd done something wrong.

'Sorry. I was being curious.' She dropped the elephant back in the ottoman.

Recognising her sudden wariness, Nikos forced a smile and made himself step over the threshold.

He hadn't set foot in this room in ten years.

He joined Marisa at the ottoman and peered down at the long-forgotten contents with a chest so tight it was like someone had trapped it in a vice. Niki took one look and started jiggling with excitement and making grabbing motions with his hands.

'Can he...?'

'No.' He curtly cut Marisa's question off before she could finish it.

She took Niki from him, her wariness more pronounced.

He grimaced and took a deep breath. The tightness and emotions bubbling in his guts were not Marisa's doing. In a more moderate tone, he said, 'This was my bedroom. This is the only thing of my childhood my mother kept.'

He'd discovered his childhood ottoman in the days after her death when sentimentality had compelled him to enter his old bedroom for the first time since he'd been taken from his parents. The rest of the room had been stripped bare. The ottoman and its contents had been the only proof in the entire villa that a child had once lived and breathed within its walls.

Nikos remembered the clear instruction he'd given the design team when he'd made the decision to renovate the place. Get rid of every piece of furniture in the villa but keep the ottoman. Keep that exactly where it is. And then he'd closed the door on his childhood bedroom and never opened it again. Not until now.

He picked up the elephant Marisa had been holding when he'd entered the room. 'This went everywhere with me.' He gave a sharp laugh and opened the dressing room door. 'Sometimes we would hide in here together when my parents were trying to kill each other.'

He looked at Marisa, rocking Niki on her hip. He turned away from the empathy shining in her eyes and looked out of the window at the guest villas in the near distance. He'd had them built over the patchwork of land that had once been his daily view.

Within a year of inheriting the place, he'd eradicated every inch of his parents' presence and his childhood from it. Apart from the ottoman.

As if reading his thoughts, she quietly asked, 'Why did you move back here?'

A pale blue sports car was approaching. His grandfather returning from his jaunt. Nikos watched it get closer while answering, 'Why would I not? It's the perfect location with all the land I could ever need.'

'But the memories…'

He faced her again and, injecting light into his voice, said, 'Memories are the past. If we allow the past to hold onto us, we can never move to the future.' To prove his point, he headed for the door, waiting for Marisa to join him so he could close it and leave the past behind, where it should be.

They walked in silence. When they reached the stairs, he caught one of her curls in his fingers. 'My grandfather is back. I'm going to talk to him about what you told me the other night. Do you want to join us?'

She shook her head. 'You go ahead. I'm going to take Niki for a swim.'

'Okay.' He cupped her cheek and placed a tender kiss to her lips before kissing their son's head. 'I'll join you when we're done.'

Marisa carried Niki to the nursery armchair and sat him on her lap. Rubbing her cheek over his soft head, she tried to swallow the choking lump in her throat.

She didn't understand why she was close to tears over an ottoman full of Nikos's old toys. Why should it affect her so deeply when it didn't matter to him?

But, if it didn't matter to him, why had he kept it? And why was that room the only unfurnished room in the whole villa?

Every time she thought she'd unlocked the mystery that was Nikos, she found another lock that needed a key.

Niki stood himself up on her lap and bounced, gurgling away happily. Wiping away a stray tear, she laughed.

'What would I do without you?' she said, putting

her mouth to his cheek and blowing on it, making him laugh manically. She blew another raspberry on his cheek and savoured the musical sound of his laughter.

Had Nikos's mother ever blown raspberries on his cheek? Had his father ever bounced him on his lap? Surely, *surely*, they had given him affection as a baby. Hadn't Nikos said his mother had used her wealth to stop his grandfather getting custody of him when he was a baby? That had to mean something.

The alternative was just too unbearable to contemplate. That Nikos could have spent his most formative years without any of the love and affection she'd been lucky enough to take for granted.

Niki stopped bouncing and rested his face in the crook of her neck. Stroking his back, she squeezed her eyes shut to stop any more tears from leaking.

Whatever love Nikos had been denied in his life, she would make up for it. Because there was no point in denying any more that she loved him. She had always loved him. And, though he might not recognise it as love and might never say the words, he loved her too. She knew it in her heart.

Sniffing back more tears, she shifted Niki higher. His head drooped. She kissed his sleeping face and gently laid him in his cot. Their swim could wait while he napped.

Making sure the baby monitor was working, Marisa crept out of the nursery and went in search of the man she loved.

\* \* \*

'They killed her father?'

Nikos swirled the last of his coffee in his mouth before swallowing it and answering his grandfather. They were sitting side by side on the terrace facing the sea, the afternoon sun beaming down on them incongruous against the darkness of their conversation. 'Yes. They tampered with the brakes of his car.'

'Why didn't you tell me this before?'

'I told you her family had suffered at the hands of the cartel.'

'But not like this.' Stratos shook his head in disbelief. 'You didn't tell me the poor child lost her father while she was pregnant with *your* child and thinking you were dead.'

The churning and twisting that had plagued Nikos's guts since he'd walked into his childhood bedroom earlier cranked up. His skin felt as if insects were crawling over it.

That damned ottoman.

Stratos continued shaking his head. 'For such a good man you have a real problem with empathy.' And then he sighed. 'I know, I know, it's something you can't help but I worry for you.'

'Your worry is misplaced,' Nikos said curtly. 'So, you will stop pretending she doesn't exist?'

'I will apologise to her… Where is she?'

'Taking Niki for a swim.' He'd intended to join them but the way he felt he would be better served taking a long swim in the sea his gaze was fixed on.

Thrashing his way through the waves would pound all these damned feelings out of him.

That damned ottoman of toys. Opening its lid had been his personal equivalent to opening Pandora's Box.

After his mother's death a decade ago, he'd closed both the door to his childhood bedroom and the door in his mind. The past was the past. What purpose did it serve to dwell on something to which he would never get any answers?

But the past had been closing in on him since his isolation and now it filled his head, cramming him with emotions and thoughts that flooded through him as if a tap had been turned on.

Why had his mother kept the ottoman when she'd got rid of all his other possessions?

Had she had latent feelings for him? A small residue of love in her heart for him?

And why had *he* kept the damn thing?

'Are you okay?' Stratos asked.

He breathed heavily and poured himself another coffee. Why was he thinking like this?

His mother and father had allowed him to be taken from them without a fight when they'd had the money and means to get him back. It was that simple. Why feel futile pangs of sentimentality over it? It was the best thing that had happened to him. If they'd wanted him back, he would have returned to a home that had bordered on a drugs den where his only love and companionship had come from a stuffed elephant.

Before his grandfather had saved him and welcomed him into his home, that stuffed elephant had been his best friend. His *only* friend. Nikos hadn't played with a single child until he was six years old. Cousins he'd had no idea existed became his playmates. *Real* playmates.

The stuffed elephant had been left behind and forgotten along with everything else.

So why the hell was he allowing it to be remembered?

The only emotion he would allow himself to feel was love for his son. In two days he would marry Marisa and he'd know that, whatever happened, his son would always have his love and protection.

He had a drink of his coffee. In no mood to hear another lecture about how his parents' neglect of him was all down to their addictions, he said, 'I was thinking about the wedding.'

'Everything is in hand?'

Nikos nodded.

'Good. I'm glad you came around to my way of thinking. When I remember the battles I had with your mother…'

Battles that had ended when Nikos passed babyhood and lost his cloak of protective cuteness, making him unlovable.

*But she had kept his toys…*

'Marriage will protect you and protect your son. Remember that. But take it from a man who knows— a miserable wife makes for a very miserable life.'

'We won't be married long enough for me to make

her miserable.' The hackles of his crawling skin rose at the look on his grandfather's face. 'A temporary marriage was *your* idea.'

'I know.' Stratos sighed. 'But that was when I thought selfishness had stopped her telling me about your son. I didn't know—'

'The decision has been made,' he interrupted curtly. An image of Marisa's beautiful face shining up at him with that softness in her eyes...

He banished it swiftly. *Theos*, his guts were cramping. His heart felt like it was tearing. 'A year of marriage is the most I can live with.'

This was what sentimentality did to you. Made you doubt yourself. Made you imagine feelings that didn't exist.

The cramping in his guts was a form of guilt, and unnecessary guilt at that.

He hadn't promised Marisa for ever. That was one lie he'd never told her.

'Time might change your mind,' Stratos said, his expression sad.

'*No*. One year and then I file for divorce.'

If time was going to change anyone's mind it would be Marisa's when she'd spent long enough with him to see whatever it was that had turned his parents away from him.

He swallowed the burn of nausea rising up his throat and again banished the image of her beautiful face from his mind...and that softness he so often saw in her eyes that, if he'd been a man who inspired love, he could almost believe was the look of love.

# CHAPTER THIRTEEN

MARISA BACKED SLOWLY to the stairs, covering her mouth tightly to stop the scream from escaping.

When she reached the top of the stairs she flew down the corridor to Seema's room and rapped loudly on it.

'Are you okay?' the nanny asked when she opened the door.

'What is the word for divorce?'

'It's *diazýgio*.'

She closed her eyes and pulled in a breath. She hadn't misunderstood. 'Thank you.'

Checking Niki was still sleeping, she hurried to her bedroom, grabbed her phone and called her sister.

Elsa answered on the third ring. 'Hi, big sister! How's Mykonos?'

'Is Santi there?'

'Yes… What's wrong?'

'Can you put him on, please? It's important.'

Seconds later, the man she'd grown up thinking of as a big brother figure was on the phone. 'What do you need?'

She swallowed her relief that he'd got straight to the point. 'Can you send one of your planes to get me?' Santi owned a fleet of planes that delivered freight across the world. He also had his own private jet.

'Are you in Mykonos?'

'Yes.'

'When do you want to be collected?'

'As soon as you can get here.'

'I will send a plane to you now. Keep your phone on you for instructions... Marisa?'

'Yes?'

'Are you okay?'

'No. But I will be. Please hurry.'

'Hold on a minute. I have a better idea. Speak to your sister while I make some calls.'

'Marisa?' This time there was panic in Elsa's voice. 'What's happened?'

'Nothing.' Yet. 'But the wedding's off. I can't marry him.'

'What's *happened*?'

'I'll tell you when I get home.' Her real home. A home filled with people who loved her. 'Do me a favour and don't tell Mama. I don't want her to worry. I'll tell her when I get back.'

'You're scaring me.'

'I promise it's nothing to scare you. He's not hurt me, I swear.' Not physically.

'You promise?'

'I promise.'

'Okay... Santi wants to talk to you again.'

There was no preamble. 'I've spoken to a contact. He's on Santorini. He's sending his jet to you now. All being well, it should land in an hour. Shall I send a car to get you to the airport?'

'Yes, please.'

'Hold tight. I'll call you when the driver's ten minutes from you. It won't be long. Hold tight,' he repeated, and then the line went dead.

Marisa didn't waste any time. Forget packing. Clothes were replaceable. Chucking her passport and Niki's into her handbag, she secured the bag over her shoulder then hurried to the nursery to pack a change-bag for Niki.

Thankfully, the ground floor was empty of people and she was able to carry Niki and their bags to the underground garage without being seen. The keys for Nikos's showroom of cars were hanging up and she pressed them all until the one with the baby seat in it flashed. She strapped a still-sleeping Niki into it before unclipping and carefully removing the seat. Rather than go back up into the house, she pressed the button to open the garage's sliding doors and waited for rescue in the shade of the terrace that ran along the side of the villa.

Her hope of being miles away before Nikos noticed they were missing was foiled a minute later when footsteps crunched behind her.

'Where are you going?'

Almost jumping out of her skin, Marisa spun around to find Nikos walking towards her.

Nikos scanned her slowly, taking in the guilt blazing on her face to the protective way she stood before their sleeping son. She couldn't have known the garage was alarmed. The moment she'd set foot in it, an alert had gone to his phone. He'd watched her every move.

'Where are you going?' he repeated icily.

She just stared at him, her face now the colour of an overripe tomato.

The faint sound of a phone buzzing broke the tense silence that developed.

'Are you not going to answer that?'

Throat moving, she slowly pulled her phone out of her handbag and put it to her ear. *'Hola.'*

The one-sided conversation in which she was required only to make the odd noise of acknowledgement was over in less than a minute. She kept her eyes on his face the entire time. He didn't think she blinked once throughout it.

Nikos folded his arms across his chest and clenched his jaw. 'Speak to me. Tell me what's going on.'

Her eyes closed. When she snapped them back open, she said in a tone that turned his blood to ice, 'I'm going home.'

Now he was the one to stare without blinking. Every part of his body tightened, his lungs squeezing into balls.

She was leaving him. He could see it in her eyes.

He'd sensed it while watching her hurried movements in the garage.

Marisa was leaving him. Her flustered guilt had

been replaced with a calm defiance he recognised from the weeks following his return. Her controlled demeanour was at complete odds with the turbulence Nikos now found himself fighting.

Hadn't he always known this day would come?

'And when were you planning to tell me?'

'I was going to send you a message.'

'A message?' Red-hot rage pulsed through him, burning through his brain. He fought to stop it echoing in his voice, speaking through gritted teeth. 'You were going to leave without a single word of warning?'

'Yes.'

She would have let him worry. Let him put out a search for her. Let him imagine the worst.

Clamping down on the rising rage that swirled with something else, something indefinable but which felt like a weight was pressing against his heart, he said, 'You have a reason?'

Contempt flashed in her eyes. 'Oh, yes.'

'Do you want to share it with me?'

She looked at her watch. 'Not really. I have a car coming.'

'A car…' He gave a quick, humourless laugh. 'You have been busy.'

'Not me. Santi. He's arranged a plane to get me home, so if you're thinking of trying to stop me leaving, you'll have him to deal with.'

'I wouldn't stop *you* leaving, *agapi mou*.' He let his gaze fall to the car seat and the child sleeping in it she was shielding with her body. 'Our son, though, is a different matter…'

She showed not the slightest hint of intimidation at the menacing words he'd deliberately left hanging.

Stepping slowly to him, she folded her arms across her chest, mimicking his stance.

Her words were delivered quietly but with absolute precision. 'I'm taking Niki home. To Valencia. To his family. To the people who have loved him since he was in my belly. And if you think you can stop me then you will learn just how dirty I'm prepared to fight.' Her face tilted. 'But I think you know that—after all, isn't that your reason for marrying me? To guarantee your access and rights to our son?'

To see the colour drain from Nikos's face stoked the fire in Marisa's belly. So her instincts *had* been right. Her Greek wasn't good enough to understand everything Nikos and his granddad had said but she'd caught enough to get the gist of it. Their body language had told her the rest.

She'd understood his reasons immediately. Understood every little part of it.

And she also understood he'd lied to her. His proposal had never been about giving Niki a stable family. It had been all about Nikos, the dirty, cruel, unconscionable *bastard*.

Moving her face as close to his as she could get without actually touching him, she summoned every muscle in her face to form a smile. 'I heard everything… Did I forget to tell you I taught myself Greek while you were playing dead? Oh, yes, I did forget…

deliberately forgot… You see, the truth is I wasn't prepared to give you the satisfaction of knowing just how desperately I grieved for you, or that my grief was so strong I had to listen to recordings of your language at night to get any sleep. That's how I found comfort. Because it was that strong.' She nodded for emphasis. 'My grief for you. I wanted to die.'

Nikos's guts fisted. The punch it made rippled straight through him.

Still speaking in that same, calm, quiet, matter-of-fact tone, she continued, 'I'm sure I would have got through that naturally with time, but the one thing that helped me cope with the grief was discovering I was pregnant.' She patted her stomach and widened her smile.

His already cold body chilled to the marrow.

'It's a real shame you missed out on the pregnancy. You never got to see my belly move or feel him kick. You missed out on the morning sickness too but I'm willing to bet you're glad about missing that part. It's funny, but only this morning I was thinking how much I would love us to have another baby and thinking that this time you could share in all of it. Not yet—I was thinking in around a year's time.' She lifted her shoulders and pulled an 'oops' face. 'That was a bit silly of me, wasn't it, what with you planning to serve me divorce papers then?'

She took a step back and shook her head in the fashion of a disappointed teacher.

'I assume you decided a year of marriage was long enough for the law to be on your side if I refused to play ball over custody arrangements? How clever you are, *mi amado*. You think of everything. I congratulate you on your deviousness.

'If only I was a poor woman, you could have gone straight for the jugular and used your wealth to get full custody without a fight. But I'm not going to fight you…' Her nostrils flared. 'Not unless you force me.' Eyes like lasers, she hissed, 'I will never stop you seeing our son but you will have to kill me before I let you take him from me. Now please excuse me, I hear a car—that will be my driver.'

She turned her back to him and leaned down to pick up the car seat.

'Are you not going to give me the courtesy of hearing me out?' Nikos asked in as modulated a tone as he could manage when he could barely hear his own voice over the roar of the heartbeats drumming in his ears. But the car coming to drive her away…he could hear that. Hear it closing in on them.

Her back to him, she retorted, 'I heard everything I needed to hear when you were talking to your grandfather.'

'So you've appointed yourself judge *and* jury?' Hooking his hands to her shoulders, he spun her round. 'This is the very reason I wanted us to marry. You think you are entitled to decide everything but you do *not* get to decide everything when it comes to our child. I'm his father.'

'You're a *liar*,' she snarled in his face. Any pretence at calm had gone. The façade she'd been wearing had dissolved like a block of salt hitting hot water. 'You said you wanted us to be a family and give Niki stability and I believed you. I swallowed my pride and did what was best for our son when all the time you were doing only what was best for yourself.'

'I was protecting my interests. How do I know you will always do what's best for him?' he demanded, his anger flaring back to life. 'Things change and people change, and I know all too well how money and power can be weaponised against a child's best interests. I was fully aware that if you decided to kick me out of our son's life, I would have an uphill battle to fight you so, yes, I lied to you, but what would you have me do? Would you have me on the fringe of our son's life waiting for the day you decide even that is too much? Without marriage, any agreement we made about access and custody would be on *your* terms. *Everything* has to be on your terms. You don't trust anyone with him. You're scared to let him out of your sight.'

'And why do you think that is?' she screamed, eyes wild. 'My life turned to hell! *I* went to hell! Your death almost killed me! Loving him saved me—he was my saving grace because he was the only part of you I had left, and I will not apologise for being over-protective, not when I spent the first eleven months of his life terrified I would lose him like I lost you and my father.'

All the fight and fury in him dissolved at the same speed hers had risen. Staring at her furiously stricken face sent the punches rippling through him harder and faster than they'd ever punched through him before.

But the fight had left her too. Tears broke through her rage and she swiped them away furiously.

'Damn you, Nikos,' she sobbed. 'Why couldn't you just leave me alone? Why did you have to do this? I never denied you any part of him. I swallowed my pride and my hate for all you'd done to me and welcomed you into our lives for Niki's sake and I made my family welcome you too, and still you think I'm just waiting for an excuse to kick you. You still see me in the same way you see everyone else—as potential hurt to be pushed aside before they can get close enough to reject you like your parents did. You think there's something wrong with you but it was never you, it was *them*. They were wrong, not you, but until you can believe that you're doomed to hurt everyone who loves you.

'I don't care how badly you were hurt as a child— you're a fully grown man who knows better than to treat people worse than dogs, but that's how you've treated *me*. How could you do this to me? Knit my heart back together and then willingly rip it apart again? Did you *ever* have feelings for me?' But then she covered her ears and staggered back. 'No. I don't want to hear it. I can't. You've broken me enough.'

The car had pulled alongside them. The driver had got out and was watching them.

Pulling her shoulders up, Marisa carried the car seat to him. 'Can you strap it in for me, please?' Her hands were shaking too much to do it herself.

About to get into the car, she turned to stare at Nikos one last time.

He hadn't moved. His features were unreadable.

Raising her chin, she swallowed and said, 'I will instruct my lawyers to draft a custody agreement when I get home. It will be as fair as it can be to all three of us.'

And then she closed the door, turned her face away from him and gazed at her son.

Niki's eyes were open. He looked at her and gave a beaming smile that melted her broken heart.

Nikos watched the car until it was no longer in sight. He couldn't make his legs move to return inside.

He sank down on the top step of the terrace and waited for the cold fog that had enveloped him to pass.

Clasping his pounding head, he swallowed hard. Everything inside him felt bruised and tight. Deep in the pit of his stomach, sickness churned, rising up his throat to leave a bitter, metallic taste in his mouth.

Time slipped away. The fog didn't clear... Not until he caught the sound of a distant car nearing. His heart thumped then everything in him slumped to realise the sound was coming from the wrong direction. A moment later, his grandfather's sports car appeared, the top down.

Stratos parked in front of Nikos and put his elbow on the lowered window. 'Everything okay?'

He managed to jerk a nod.

'You're sure?'

Another nod. He cleared his throat. 'Where are you going?'

'Poker night at Stelios'. We're having food first. I tried to find Marisa to apologise but I couldn't find her. I'll talk to her tomorrow.' He put the car back into gear. 'Got to go—I'm already late. Don't wait up,' he added with a cackle, then drove off in the same direction Marisa had not long travelled.

For an octogenarian, his grandfather had a re-markable social life. A string of women. Raucous nights out with good company. The kind of social life Nikos had looked forward to resuming after his resurrection. The kind he would have if he hadn't learned about his son.

He blinked. What was he thinking?

Hadn't he stayed out of the spotlight and avoided any kind of socialising until he'd seen Marisa again? Hadn't he embedded himself back into her life?

The only times he'd enjoyed himself after his re-turn from the dead had been with her because the vacuous social scene he'd once revelled in no longer meant anything to him. His isolation had changed him. Marisa had changed him. His son had changed him.

And how had he learned about his son? By fol-lowing the mother. Why had he followed the mother? Because the compulsion to see her one last time had been too strong to resist...

Fighting the direction of his thoughts and unable to look a moment longer at the road on which she'd travelled away from him, Nikos dragged himself to his feet and walked back into his home.

The emptiness was stark.

The silence was deafening.

He held tight to the bannister and climbed both flights of stairs without any thought of where he was heading.

Shuffling along the corridor on the second floor, the nausea in his stomach rose up like a wave. He doubled over, pressing his hands to the sill of the window he was passing to support himself, and closed his eyes.

When the sickness passed, he opened his eyes and found his gaze drawn back to the winding road in the distance. His grandfather's car had disappeared.

He straightened sharply as clarity exploded into his thoughts.

His grandfather wasn't the one who needed to apologise to Marisa. His antipathy had been a direct consequence of Nikos's actions. If he'd opened up to Marisa all that time ago about his life, she would have understood what his grandfather meant to him and reached out to Stratos, however deep her despair had been.

But he hadn't opened up. He couldn't change that. Couldn't change who he was. Couldn't change that he never opened up to anyone…

But hadn't he opened up to Marisa? It had been forced on him but he *had* opened up to her, about virtually everything.

She knew him better than anyone else. When he'd

given her his blasé reason for moving into this villa the look in her eyes had told him she understood the real reason behind it, even if it was one he'd never acknowledged to himself, that he'd moved back here to prove to himself that the past didn't affect him when the ottoman's very existence proved otherwise. Marisa had seen that. And still she'd given him that same soft smile of love.

Yes, love.

Whatever it was that had stopped his parents loving him hadn't stopped Marisa placing her cheek to his chest and listening to the beats of his heart…

The beats of his heart picked up speed and he looked at his old bedroom door. That's where he'd been heading, he now realised, but what he'd intended to do in there he didn't know, just knew it no longer mattered. If he wanted a future then he had to free himself from the shackles of the past. Free himself properly. In his heart.

Having his child growing inside Marisa had given her comfort. When she'd described grief as being a bruise that hurts with every breath you take, she'd been speaking about her grief for *him*. How had he not seen that?

Because he'd never thought for a second that he could inspire such feelings in anyone.

When he'd hidden in the shadows for eighteen months, hers had been the face he'd seen before falling asleep. Hadn't he done the same as she'd done in those long months apart? Listened to recordings of *her* language to help him sleep?

*Theos*, he saw it so clearly now. *Understood* so clearly.

Marisa had been the reason he'd taken the extreme action of faking his own death. To protect her. Because, even then, the thought of anyone or anything harming her in any way had been unbearable and he'd preferred to die himself than expose her to any danger.

Patting his pockets, he found his phone and, fighting the panic threatening to overwhelm him, quickly scrolled through the contacts.

'Thodoris?' he said when his call was answered. 'It's Nikos Manolas. I need your help.'

# CHAPTER FOURTEEN

NIKI HAD BEEN amazingly well behaved on the flight over to Mykonos. Unfortunately, the return journey was yet to go so smoothly. He'd taken one look at the plane at the private airfield they were flying from and started bawling. He was still bawling and the plane hadn't even taken off. Marisa soothed him as much as she could but all her bribes of food and drink—she kept emergency ready-made baby food and baby milk in the change-bag—went to waste.

Picking him up and pacing the cabin while rubbing his back, she asked the cabin crew the reason for the delay. They'd been ready to take off for twenty minutes. None of the crew knew or, if they did, weren't sharing the reasons with her.

She sat down again and made another attempt at giving Niki milk. This time he accepted it and quietened.

Marisa soon wished he would become fractious again. Resting her head back against the leather seat, she squeezed her eyes shut and tried to banish Nikos's face from her mind. Tried to ignore the unbearable pain in her heart. Tried to banish the tempest of emotions swelling inside her. Tried to stop the force of the painful ragged rise and fall of her chest from pushing out the tears forming behind her eyes. It would have been easier to stop the sun from rising. They fell down her face like a burning stream.

Her hands full with feeding Niki, she couldn't wipe the tears away, and she turned her face to the window to stop them falling onto him and tried her hardest to get control of herself. She didn't want her devastation to feed into Niki's developing emotions. She *must* keep hold of herself until she was in the security of her home and the privacy of her bedroom. She could fall apart then, just as she'd done during those desolate months and months spent believing Nikos to be dead. Pack her emotions back inside her.

'Are you okay?' One of the cabin crew was hovering beside her, clearly concerned.

She gave a jerky nod, and something she hoped was a smile, but couldn't open her mouth for fear the anguish would pour out of it.

Turning back to look out of the window, she saw through the film of tears clouding her vision something large and black approaching.

She blinked vigorously then found herself freezing when her vision cleared enough to recognise the object. It was a car. One of Nikos's cars.

She blinked again to see him jump out of the front passenger seat before the car had even come to a stop.

His long legs sped in a blur towards the plane.

Moments later and he was in the cabin and striding over to her.

His eyes locked straight onto hers. His Adam's apple moved up and down his throat repeatedly before his lips finally parted.

'Don't leave me,' he said in a hoarse voice.

She could only stare at him. Was this really Nikos? Was this wild-eyed, dishevelled man the same perfectly groomed and contained man she'd left only an hour ago?

His frantic eyes held hers. There was a sheen in them...

And then she remembered what an excellent actor he'd already proved himself to be and turned her face away. 'Go home, Nikos. I've already said we can make an agreement for custody that's fair to all of us. You've nothing to worry about. I won't stop you seeing Niki.'

'This is nothing to do with our son. Please, Marisa, I am begging you... Don't go.'

'Why?' she asked tonelessly.

'Because I can't live without you.'

Thinking she might be sick at the new lows he'd just plumbed, she snapped her face back to him. 'You sick, lying bastard.'

Nikos winced but accepted the deserved blow. 'I am a bastard. I've treated you appallingly but I'm...' He took a deep breath and pulled viciously at his hair. 'Can you give Niki to one of the crew? There are things I need to say that I don't want him to hear.'

Her red eyes—*Theos*, his cruelty had caused

that—narrowed but after a moment she rose from her seat and carried Niki to the door behind which the cabin crew stayed.

Nikos sank into the seat opposite the one she'd been sitting in and bowed his head, scraping his nails over the back of his skull, trying to gather his thoughts before she returned.

His thoughts were still splintered when she sat down again.

He lifted his head.

Her legs were crossed, spine straight, an imperious expression on her blotchy, tear-stained face. He recognised that expression. It was the one she'd used in the weeks after he'd broken her heart when he'd brazenly confessed to having had no intention of telling her to her face that he was alive. Why hadn't he recognised her stance as a protective shield?

'My grandfather told me earlier that I lack empathy,' he said slowly, the answer to his own question coming to him.

'He is not wrong.'

'He is. To a degree.'

She arched a brow in response.

'I learned at a young age to block feelings.'

'I've already guessed that. And you have my sympathy for the reasons behind it.'

'I don't want your sympathy.'

'I know that too.'

'I can stop my heart from feeling. Turn it to stone.'

'To stop yourself from being hurt again. You don't need to be Freud to understand that, Nikos.'

He nodded his agreement. 'It stops me being hurt but it also stops me being able to recognise other people's pain.' He grimaced and corrected himself. 'Rather, it enables me to *ignore* their pain, even the pain of those who are close to me.' He gave a grunt of gloomy laughter. 'Not that I have let anyone get close to me, not even my grandfather—even from him I can separate my heart. I lived in England for seven years and barely thought of him. Can you believe that? That man saved me, put up with all my rebellions and I treated him like that?'

'You've made up for it with him.'

He felt a tiny release of the pressure on his chest at this slight softening.

'And then I met you.'

She stiffened.

'Marisa… You…' He pinched the bridge of his nose and swallowed. 'I don't know why it was different with you but there is something about you I reacted to more strongly than I have ever reacted to anyone before. I have never craved someone's company before and it was never just about the sex, even if I did try to kid myself that that's all it was. I told myself your words of love to me were just words. How could you love me, someone so inherently unlovable his parents let him go without a fight?

'But you would put your cheek to my chest and I'd know you were listening to my heartbeat. You wanted to feel *my* heartbeat. No one had ever done that before. No one had ever got close enough to. And I would feel your heartbeat against my skin too and the warmth of your body and just want to stay there and never let you go.'

The imperious expression on Marisa's face had gone.

'I think I fell in love with you a long time ago and didn't know it. But even if I had, I would have fought it and the outcome would have been the same. I would have still faked my death without telling you and with no intention of resuming our affair because it was safer for me. You'd got too close… Every day of our affair lived in me the fear that you would see whatever was rotten in me that my parents had seen and push me aside without another thought.

'When I found that photograph of you in the pile of photos of my lawyer's dead body…' He closed his eyes and sucked in a breath. 'That was the first time I'd felt real terror since I was taken from my parents and it was a thousand times worse. That was the thing that pushed me over the edge into faking my death. I needed to protect you. I insisted on daily reports about you. I could only sleep at night if I knew you were safe. When I learned what had happened to your father… *Theos*, my terror for you…'

Her eyes glistened. Her chin was wobbling, throat moving.

'Once it was all over, I never wanted to see you again. You'd made me feel things, *agapi mou*, and that terrified me. Feelings leave you vulnerable. It's perverse logic, I know, but subconsciously I knew if I pushed you away first then you couldn't leave me. You couldn't hurt me.'

A tear rolled down her cheek. He wanted so badly to press his thumb to her cheek and brush the tear away.

'I tried to stay away from you. I even told myself the day I waited outside your estate that all I wanted was one last glimpse as a private goodbye. If it hadn't been for Niki, you wouldn't have seen me again but he was the excuse I needed to justify throwing myself back into your life and even then I fought it. I fell in love with our son and I could accept that love because he was an innocent child who could never hurt me, whereas you... Marisa, you have no idea of the power you have over me. You have no idea how much it tortured me to imagine you with Raul. I thought you'd moved on—how could you not? How could I be special enough for anyone to grieve?

'But I never moved on from you. It was impossible.'

The beats of Marisa's heart were so strong the echoes thrashed in her dazed, barely comprehending head. The desperation with which she wanted to believe him...

But the *fear*.

She shrank back as he slid onto the floor to kneel before her and shrank into herself when he took her hand. She tried to block her ears to his words, deny them their power.

'There is only you,' he said quietly. 'And I can't fight it any more or deny it to myself. I love you. You have turned my stone-cold heart into something that beats freely with love for you. It's *you* I need to be with. *You* I need to spend my nights with. *You* I trust with my life, my soul and my heart. Please, give me one more chance, let me prove myself to be the man you deserve, I beg you, and not for our son's sake but for mine because I can't live without you. I've tried and every road leads back to you. Let me earn your love and your trust. I swear on our son's life that I will never betray it again. I swear.'

Marisa barely noticed her fingers had laced into his. The seams of her ripped, damaged heart were threading hesitantly back together and, finally, she dared to look at him. 'When I agreed to marry you, it was for Niki's sake.'

He breathed deeply. 'I know.'

'Everything I've done since I learned I was pregnant has been for him.'

His voice became a hoarse whisper. 'I know.'

'But you…' She leaned forward, closer to him. 'You brought me back to life. You made me remember that I'm not just a mother but a woman with needs of her own. And that woman loves you,' she whispered. 'She's always loved you.'

His throat moved. 'I never deserved it. But I will. If you'll let me.'

Hands shaking, she cupped his cheeks and stared deeper into his eyes. The look she saw in them sewed the last piece of her heart back into place.

'Yes.' Unable to contain the feelings a moment longer, she brought her face to his and kissed him. 'Oh, Nikos, yes.'

He made a sound like a prayer and then his arms

wrapped tightly around her and she was enveloped in his arms so tenderly and lovingly that her mended heart soared into song.

Nikos stared into Marisa's eyes, filled to the brim with emotions. And when she smiled and said, 'Let's get our son and go home,' he knew he would spend the rest of his life worshipping her and thanking God every day for bringing her into his life and setting him free to love. To love her.

# EPILOGUE

NIKOS STOOD BACK and admired his handiwork. He'd spent the weekend in his 'man cave', as his wife called it, sanding and repainting his childhood ottoman. It looked brand new. He liked to think his son would be thrilled with it but knowing Niki, he would think of it only as an excellent new space for when he played hide-and-seek with his sister. And that was okay. More than okay.

Childhood was precious and his children would one day grow into adulthood with the happiest of memories to look back on, and this ottoman that had witnessed so much trauma would now be nestled in a home filled with love. It had been reborn, just as he had been.

The man cave door opened and Marisa appeared. She slipped an arm around his waist and pressed herself close to him. 'You've done an amazing job,' she said softly. 'Are you pleased with it?'

He kissed the top of her head and pressed his cheek into her hair. 'Yes. Thank you for not letting me set fire to it.'

She squeezed her arms around him. No further words were needed.

He remembered how she'd found him months after their wedding, about to place it on the fire-pit, thinking it needed to be done to set the past free in its entirety. How she'd wrapped her arms around him, much as she was holding him now, and quietly asked if he was sure he wanted to burn the only solid reminder of his mother's love for him.

'For all her sins and neglect, she did love you, Nikos,' she'd said. 'And if you ever still doubt that, look at this ottoman and remember that deep in her heart, whether she acknowledged it to herself or not, she couldn't bear to lose all of you. She kept a part of you with her. Now it's for you to keep a part of her with you.'

It had taken a further four years for him to set to work on it. Four years of unconditional love from the woman he would give his life for. Four years of happiness that had flushed the pain of his childhood from him until all that was left was a rare kernel of melancholy.

For a long time they stood in silence, doing nothing but stare at the object of his past brought into their present to be a part of their lives for ever.

'Mama, Mama!'

The voice of their son carried through the air and they left the man cave to find five-year-old Niki racing to them. His three-year-old sister, Rose, ran after him, cheeks puffing, arms pumping as she tried valiantly to keep pace with her adored big brother.

Niki's light brown eyes were alight as he breathlessly said, 'Aunty Elsa and Uncle Santi are here.'

Golden-haired Rose threw her arms around Nikos's knees and stared up at him with the same bright-eyed excitement. 'Baby Marco here too!'

Holding their children's hands, they headed off to welcome their house guests and fill their home with even more love and laughter.

\* \* \* \* \*

*Wrapped up in*
The Secret Behind the Greek's Return*?*

*You're sure to love the first instalment of the*
*Billion-Dollar Mediterranean Brides duet*
The Forbidden Innocent's Bodyguard

*Why not also explore these other stories*
*by Michelle Smart?*

Her Sicilian Baby Revelation
Her Greek Wedding Night Debt
A Baby to Bind His Innocent
The Billionaire's Cinderella Contract
The Cost of Claiming His Heir

*Available now!*

## #3937 CINDERELLA'S DESERT BABY BOMBSHELL
*Heirs for Royal Brothers*
by Lynne Graham

Penniless Tatiana Hamilton must marry Prince Saif after his original bride, her cousin, disappears. The ice-cold sheikh promises to end their sham marriage quickly. Until their chemistry grows too hot to ignore...and Tati discovers she's pregnant!

## #3938 A CONSEQUENCE MADE IN GREECE
by Annie West

Cora thinks she knows Strato's rich, privileged type. But the man she uncovers during their no-strings encounters is captivating. A man whose past made him swear never to marry or become a father—and whose baby she's now carrying...

## #3939 NINE MONTHS TO TAME THE TYCOON
*Innocent Summer Brides*
by Chantelle Shaw

Their blazing chemistry was more than enough to tempt Lissa into her first night of sensual abandon with Takis. Now she's pregnant... and he's demanding they turn one night into marriage vows!

## #3940 THE SICILIAN'S FORGOTTEN WIFE
by Caitlin Crews

Innocent Josselyn agreed to marry dangerously compelling Cenzo, unaware of his desire for revenge against her family. But when an accident causes him to forget everything—except their electrifying chemistry—the tables are turned...

## #3941 THE WEDDING NIGHT THEY NEVER HAD
by Jackie Ashenden

As king, Cassius requires a real queen by his side. Not Inara, his wife in name only. But when their unfulfilled desire finally gives her the courage to ask for a true marriage, can Inara be the queen he needs?

## #3942 MANHATTAN'S MOST SCANDALOUS REUNION
*The Secret Sisters*
by Dani Collins

When the paparazzi mistake Nina for a supermodel, she takes refuge in her ex's New York penthouse. Big mistake. She's reminded of just how intensely seductive Reve can be. And how difficult it will be to walk away...again.

## #3943 BEAUTY IN THE BILLIONAIRE'S BED
by Louise Fuller

Guarded billionaire Arlo Milburn never expected to find gorgeous stranger Frankie Fox in his bed! While they're stranded on his private island, their intense attraction brings them together... But can it break down his walls entirely?

## #3944 THE ONLY KING TO CLAIM HER
*The Kings of California*
by Millie Adams

Innocent queen Annick knows there are those out there looking to destroy her. Turning to dark-hearted Maximus King is the answer, but she's shocked when he proposes a much more permanent solution—marriage!

---

"I wish only to kiss my wife," Cenzo growled. "On this, the first day of the rest of our life together."

"You don't want to kiss me." She threw the words at him, and he thought the way she trembled now was her temper taking hold. "You want to start what you think will be my downward spiral, until all I can do is fling myself prostrate before you and cringe about at your feet. Guess what? I would rather die."

"Let us test that theory," he suggested and kissed her.

And this time, it had nothing at all to do with punishment. Though it was no less a claiming.

This time, it was a seduction.

Pleasure and dark promise.

He took her face in his hands, and he tasted her as he'd wanted at last. He teased her lips until she sighed, melting against him, and opened to let him in.

He kissed her and he kissed her, until all that fury, all that need, hummed there between them. He kissed her, losing himself in the sheer wonder of her taste and the way that sweet-sea scent of hers teased at him, as if she was bewitching him despite his best efforts to seize control.

Cenzo kissed her like a man drowning, and she met each thrust of his tongue, then moved closer as if she was as greedy as he was.

As if she knew how much he wanted her and wanted him, too, with that very same intensity.

And there were so many things he wanted to do with her. But kissing her felt like a gift, like sheer magic, and for once in his life, Cenzo lost track of his own ulterior motives. His own grand plan.

There was only her taste. Her heat.

Her hair, which he gripped with his hands, and the way she pressed against him.

There was only Josselyn. His wife.

He kissed her again and again, and then he shifted, meaning to lift her in his arms—

But she pushed away from him, enough to brace herself against his chest. He found his hands on her upper arms.

"I agreed to marry you," she panted out at him, her lips faintly swollen and her brown eyes wild. "I refuse to be a pawn in your game."

"You can be any piece on the board that you like," he replied, trying to gather himself. "But it will still be my board, Josselyn."

He let her go, lifting up his hands theatrically. "By all means, little wife. Run and hide if that makes you feel more powerful."

He kept his hands in the air, his mock surrender, and laughed at her as he stepped back.

Because he'd forgotten, entirely, that they stood on those narrow stairs.

It was his own mocking laughter that stayed with him as he fell, a seeming slow-motion slide backward when his foot encountered only air. He saw her face as the world fell out from beneath him.

*Don't miss*
The Sicilian's Forgotten Wife
*available September 2021 wherever*
*Harlequin Presents books and ebooks are sold.*

Harlequin.com

HPEXP0821

# *Love Harlequin romance?*

## DISCOVER.

Be the first to find out about promotions,
news and exclusive content!

Facebook.com/HarlequinBooks

Twitter.com/HarlequinBooks

Instagram.com/HarlequinBooks

Pinterest.com/HarlequinBooks

YouTube.com/HarlequinBooks

ReaderService.com

## EXPLORE.

Sign up for the Harlequin e-newsletter and
download a free book from any series at
**TryHarlequin.com**

## CONNECT.

Join our Harlequin community to
share your thoughts and connect
with other romance readers!
**Facebook.com/groups/HarlequinConnection**

HSOCIAL2021